P9-DYZ-904

West of Washoe

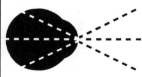

This Large Print Book carries the
Seal of Approval of N.A.V.H.

WEST OF WASHOE

A WESTERN STORY

TIM CHAMPLIN

THORNDIKE PRESS
A part of Gale, Cengage Learning

GALE
CENGAGE Learning™

Detroit • New York • San Francisco • New Haven, Conn • Waterville, Maine • London

GALE
CENGAGE Learning

Thorndike Press® Large Print Western.
The text of this Large Print edition is unabridged.
Other aspects of the book may vary from the original edition.
Set in 16 pt. Plantin.
Printed on permanent paper.

LIBRARY OF CONGRESS CATALOGING-IN-PUBLICATION DATA

Champlin, Tim, 1937–
   West of Washoe : a western story / by Tim Champlin.
      p. cm. — (Thorndike Press large print western)
   ISBN-13: 978-1-4104-1865-4 (alk. paper)
   ISBN-10: 1-4104-1865-0 (alk. paper)
   1. Mining engineers—Fiction. 2. Virginia City
(Nev.)—History—Fiction. 3. Large type books. I. Title.
PS3553.H265W45 2009b
813'.54—dc22   2009017528

Published in 2009 by arrangement with Golden West Literary Agency.

Printed in the United States of America
1 2 3 4 5 6 7 13 12 11 10 09

Health and Happiness
To My Brother, Patrick,
Who is skilled at many things.

CHAPTER ONE

"Hyah!"

Gil Ross was jarred out of a sound sleep as the coach lunged ahead. His eyes flew open. Blackness. Whistles and shouts came from the box as the driver cracked his whip, urging the six-horse hitch to a gallop.

Ross was irritated at being rudely awakened. But sudden instinct rang an alarm bell. *What was going on?*

Before he could reach to yank aside the canvas curtain by the coach window, a hole exploded in the right side door panel and a load of buckshot slammed into the empty middle bench seat.

"Damn!" He jerked back, stray pellets stinging his shin.

The woman beside him screamed, and Ross pulled her down behind him on the leather seat, fearing the next shot would come through the window.

"My God, we'll all be killed!" the fat

whiskey drummer cried, cringing into the opposite corner of the coach.

In one smooth motion, Ross slid his Navy Colt from its holster and went to one knee on the floor, pulling back the window drape.

Cold rain was slashing sideways. A muzzle flash stabbed the blackness and he snapped off a shot in that direction. Shouts and curses were punctuated by gunfire. Vague, moving forms of horses were receding in the murk. He flinched as a bullet struck splinters from the window sill by his cheek.

He fired twice more at muzzle flashes, then emptied his six-shot revolver in the general direction of the riders pursuing them. The blurred forms disappeared from his vision, swallowed up in the blackness behind, as the coach picked up speed, rocking and pitching on the narrow road. Wet tree limbs whipped past his face, and he pulled back from the window. He could hear rifle fire from atop the coach, so the guard still had the attackers in sight.

A long half minute passed, and the firing from above ceased. Ross moved to the other side, and looked out, but could see nothing. Bracing himself against the wild motion of the coach, he waited another two minutes, wishing he could see well enough to reload his Navy Colt with black powder.

"Are they still out there?" The woman's voice was shaky.

"I think they gave it up." Ross had no way of knowing, but wanted to reassure her. "Anybody hurt?" he asked, holstering his gun.

"No," she said, a little more calmly. "Just scared out of my wits."

"I'm not hit," the drummer replied.

Ross fingered a match from his vest pocket and raked it against the wood paneling. He squinted against the flare, then held the steady flame to examine the damage to his shin just above the boot top. A few pellets had raked the skin, drawing a trickle of blood.

"Oh, you're wounded!" The match went out and he heard her scuffing in the dark. "Here, pour a little of this on it." She pressed a small flask into his hand. He pulled the stopper and sniffed. Whiskey. "Thanks." He splashed a little onto his fingers and rubbed it on his shin, feeling the satisfying sting of alcohol. "Maybe I should have taken the day coach," he muttered, handing back the flask.

"Then you wouldn't have been here to defend us," she said, turning up the flask for a nip before slipping it into her handbag. "I thought this night run would be safer, too," she said. "Had a hard time finding out about this coach."

"The company doesn't advertise," Ross said. "They try to make irregular, unannounced runs at night across the Sierras to avoid hold-ups. Seems like every coach to or from Washoe to Sacramento and the Coast is carrying bullion, coin, or personal valuables."

"The day coaches are a lot more crowded," she added. "And I hear tell they're robbed even more often. Guess these robbers can see better in daylight. They don't seem to have any fear of being shot or caught."

"Reckon they figure it's worth the risk since nearly all the coaches are carrying treasure."

The driver had not slowed the team. The heavy Concord leaned precariously into a curve, its spinning wheels skidding sideways in the muddy ruts of the mountain road. The woman was thrown against him. A second later, the six-horse hitch jerked the careening coach upright, and they plunged ahead out of the turn.

"Sorry." She pushed herself upright, grabbing the window sill to steady herself.

"No need to apologize," he said, savoring her scented presence.

Ross hoped they'd finally outrun or discouraged the gunmen. Or were these attackers working in groups, running the coach into an ambush up ahead, in the manner of hunting lions? He was thankful he'd packed a loaded back-up gun for any last-ditch emergencies. The weapon — a Smith & Wesson .32 cartridge revolver — had a four-inch barrel and fit snugly in the inside pocket of his coat.

Pulling aside the canvas curtain, Ross squinted against rain that was turning to stinging sleet as they ascended into colder mountain air. *Black as the inside of my boot,* he thought. *Where are we?* Jagged lightning ripped the darkness, its brief glare revealing the tops of wildly thrashing pines in the cañon below. The edge of the road fell away barely three feet from the flying hoofs of their team. Blinding light winked out and his senses were numbed by a cannonade of thunder that *boomed* from rock wall to timbered cañon, drowning the drum roll of hoof beats and the *rattle* of trace chains.

"Hyah! Hyah!" The cries and *popping* of the driver's whip sounded faintly on the gusting crosswind as the coach hurtled along at liver-curling speed somewhere east of Placerville and west of Washoe, bound for Virginia City. The highwaymen had some-

how found out about this run. Ross had to assume they also knew the coach was burdened with bags of freshly minted gold and silver coins from the San Francisco mint.

"We got past those road agents, but now that damned driver's gonna run us off into one these cañons and kill us, sure," the whiskey drummer whined.

"Not likely," Ross said, even though his own stomach was tensing. "A good team of horses, given their head, can hold a familiar road in the dark or blinding snow, even when the driver can't see the wheelers' tails." He hoped his manner had a calming affect because he knew the team's leaders were being severely tested tonight. "Besides, don't you know who's up there, handling the ribbons? It's Frank Moody, the best driver on the Pioneer Line." He gestured at the woman passenger in the dark. "If this lady isn't scared, why should you be?"

"Yeah," the drummer growled. "But all the same, I wish we were in Virginia City."

"Come daylight, we will be." He felt he had to say something further, thinking a confident tone might allay the man's uneasiness. "That hold-up try was really stupid. Or maybe those gunmen were just overconfident, thinking they could stop this coach and challenge the guard in the middle of a wild storm. They'll never catch us now. Moody's driving like those lightning bolts are flaming pitchforks from hell."

A few minutes later, the coach began to slow and Ross sensed the long grade was steepening.

"Whoa!"

The coach came to a halt, rocking gently on its leather thorough braces.

Ross climbed out, leaving the other two inside. If there was enough illumination from the side lanterns of the coach, he'd reload his Colt. There wasn't.

Wrapping the reins around the brake handle, Moody stepped down. The guard remained on the box, shoving cartridges into the loading tube under the barrel of his Henry rifle.

"Everybody all right?" Moody asked in a rolling bass voice. Ross saw only the faint white blob of Moody's linen duster as the driver came around to check on the woman passenger still inside.

A gust from the valley behind them brought the cold, damp smell of rain. Small pellets of sleet bounced off Ross's hat brim. He shivered. The wind was getting up on its hind legs, he thought, listening to the roar in the tops of the giant ponderosas. He'd heard that sound before — in the rigging of a brigantine off Cape Horn.

A flicker of lightning illuminated the scene in stark, white light.

"Son-of-a-bitch!" Moody exploded. Then quickly added: "Apologies, ma'am."

Ross saw the reason for his anger. The varnished door paneling, on which was painted a peaceful scene of the Lakes of Killarney, now bore a ragged hole the size of a saucer.

Moody muttered something under his breath, damning all robbers to perdition. He went around the coach, checking the leather tie-down on the rear luggage boot, giving a tug on each muddy wheel to be sure everything was secure. He pulled off his gloves and walked forward to the team, stroking each horse, speaking softly in his soothing voice. The animals were blowing and tossing their heads, hides and breath steaming.

A mixture of cold raindrops and sleet began to spatter down as Moody came back.

"How'd you get past 'em?" Ross asked.

"By God, I'd had enough and decided this time it was them or me," Moody declared, removing his big hat and wiping a sleeve across his face. "When they yelled to hold up, I just ducked down and yelled at the guard to let 'em have it. Whipped up the team and tried to run down that s.o.b. who was afoot in the middle of the road. Reckon he thought we'd stop when he had the drop on us. But it was dark and raining and I figured our chances were as good as his. But he was faster than the horses and hopped outta the way and cut loose with a shotgun as we went past. Glad nobody inside was hit."

Ross didn't bother to mention the buckshot that'd raked his leg.

"Once we got the jump, they couldn't ride alongside 'cause the road's too narrow and lined with trees," Moody went on. "Near as I could tell there were three or four of 'em." He paused and looked back down the dark road. "I think they've given it up as a bad job tonight. They ain't too smart or they would've waylaid us at the top of the grade when the horses were winded." He looked at Ross in the dim light of the side lantern. "What's your name?"

"Gil Ross."

"Ross, thanks for lending us a dose or two of hot lead to help fend 'em off."

"Wish I had a rifle."

"Next time, bring one." Moody put a boot on the front wheel hub and swung up to this lofty seat. "Get aboard and hang on. We'll make some time."

Ross pulled off his long, woolen scarf and stuffed it into the hole in the door to keep out the cold and wet. He boarded and slammed the door just as the coach lurched ahead, throwing him back into the seat.

Ross peered into the dimness, trying to get a good look at the woman. She'd come aboard at the Strawberry Valley station while he was dozing. Now, wrapped in her traveling cloak, her feet encased in high-buttoned shoes and propped on a carpetbag, she leaned into the far corner. Except for her initial fright, she seemed pretty self-assured, and he couldn't help but wonder what business was taking her to the mining towns and why she was traveling alone — possibly to get work in one of the sporting houses in Virginia City or Gold Hill or Carson? Only last year, soiled doves had been brought in by the coach load to fill the demand. He wondered if things had settled down some. This was his second trip to Virginia City. In the spring of 1860, lacking roads and available transportation, he'd shouldered a pack and hiked over the mountains, following the flood of prospectors rushing to get in on the new silver strikes. He'd not gone in search of precious metal, but was sent by *Harper's Weekly* to report on the new diggings, the first major boom in more than ten years. Although this was primarily a silver rush, enough gold was mixed in the ore to keep the price of mine stock fluctuating wildly.

Four long years had passed since his first visit, and apparently things were now considerably changed. Groups of enterprising men had graded toll roads on certain stretches to level out the old trails. Trains of pack mules were replaced by lumbering freight wagons and regular stagecoach service. Deep shafts and drifts were dug and timbered. Heavy hoisting equipment was hauled in. Miners who worked for hourly wages on shifts around the clock were now digging and blasting out tons of ore to be crushed by pounding stamp mills. Ingots of rich metal were molded, crated, and hauled in heavy wagons over the mountains to San Francisco.

Speculation was rampant. If newspaper accounts and rumors could be believed, paupers one day were millionaires the next, then paupers the following week. The lowliest clerks and barmaids and stable hands traded mining stock on a daily basis, fleecing one another and outsiders with regularity. To Ross, it was amazing. The heavy blue mud that'd clogged the sluices of early gold placer miners had turned out to be the richest silver ore on earth.

Now he was returning — not as a magazine reporter, but as an employee of the federal government, inspecting the potential richness of the region's mines. There was little pressure on him to hurry, since statehood would soon be a fact. President Lincoln reportedly wanted the wealth and votes of the new state of Nevada for the Union. With or without Ross's report, statehood would be assured before the fall election.

Political connections — a California senator was a personal friend — had landed him this job. But critics of the spoils system couldn't cry too loudly, since Ross was qualified for the position by two years of college geology and a year of practical experience as a miner.

Ross's wife was dead of typhus, and his two children grown and on their own, so he was concerned only with supporting himself. It wasn't difficult, but his life was rather lonely. That was one reason he caught himself looking with interest at any reasonably attractive female he came across in his travels. Whether they looked back was another matter. He flattered himself that he appeared younger than his actual age of forty-seven. The fact that he went against current fashion by remaining clean-shaven strengthened the impression of youthfulness.

The coach lurched into a hole and he grabbed for the hanging strap with one hand. How long before they came down out of these mountains? He was confident Moody knew his business and had driven this road several hundred times in all kinds of weather, winter and summer. But anyone could make a miscalculation. Constant dampness could have rotted a leather thorough brace, an axle could break, or a wheel could ride a few inches over the lip of a washed-out trail, sending the coach tumbling and splintering into a ravine. The possibilities were nothing he cared to ponder.

In spite of his edginess, Ross sagged with fatigue — a reaction from the attack. He didn't want to strike a match to look at his watch, and didn't much care what time it was as he braced his muddy boots against the damaged middle bench and sought oblivion in a corner. Hat over his eyes, he gradually drifted off to sleep.

Some time later, he came partially awake, heard voices outside, and realized the coach had stopped. He listened long enough to know they were only changing horses at a swing station. He squirmed into a more comfortable position and dozed off again.

Chapter Two

A sudden deceleration threw Ross forward, jolting him from sleep. Brakes were grinding against iron wheel rims. He sat up and stretched, looking out the crack beside the curtain. They were rolling down the last steep grade to the gentler slopes toward Gold Hill and Virginia City. It was dawn.

The drummer opposite still slept, head lolling against the seat back, mouth slack. The woman saw he was awake and gave him a tired smile, eyes puffy. He was glad finally to get a clearer look at her. Under better circumstances, her beauty would have been striking — smooth skin, full, pouty lips, fine bone structure. But nobody looked good this time of morning. Ross nodded to her. His own eyes were gritty, his mouth sour. He was glad the night had passed and they were descending the foothills.

He rolled up the curtain beside him and tied it. The chill spring air was at least fresh from the staleness of human breath, damp wool, and the dried sweat of fear. Ross drew his Navy Colt, put it on half cock, and turned the cylinder to check the loads. Empty. If a man went armed, as most did, it was wise to keep his weapon loaded and capped. He retrieved the small handgrip from beneath his feet. Among the items he kept with him were a brass flask of black powder, a cotton sack of .36-caliber lead balls, two tins of copper percussion caps, and a little jar of grease. With all the rain and dampness, it was good to have fresh loads to make sure his powder was dry and wouldn't misfire. Not that he was expecting to have to use his pistol as soon as he got off the stage, but it was best to be prepared.

Out of the corner of his eye, he noticed the woman watching him. He finished, eased the hammer down between chambers for safety, and holstered his weapon. She smiled at him, holding out his scarf that she'd pulled from the hole in the door. "You might need this," she said.

"Thanks."

"Thank you for keeping us dry."

Ross didn't try to widen the conversational opening. He would never see this woman again when they disembarked. He was tired and hungry and wanted most of all to get breakfast, soak in a hot tub of water, and sleep, in that order.

Forty minutes later Frank Moody reined them to a stop in front of the Virginia City stage depot. The three passengers climbed out to reclaim their luggage.

As Ross waited for the driver to unlace the rear boot, he ran an eye over the Concord. Covered with mud clear up to the windows. The horses' legs and flanks were in the same sorry condition. Even Moody's white linen duster was spattered with muddy water.

"Sorry about all that excitement, folks," Moody said, handing out their valises. "But it turned out all right, except for a little scuffing of the coach." He smiled as cheerfully as if he'd just arisen from a good night's sleep. *And well he might,* Ross thought. *The driver is in line for a bonus. Since Wells, Fargo guarantees every shipment, big or small, Moody and the guard had just risked their lives to save the company the loss of many thousands of dollars. Luck had played a part, as it usually did in any endeavor, but with these night shipments it was company property first, employees and passengers second.*

"Well, I definitely got my money's worth," Ross said, shouldering his bedroll. He glanced up and saw the guard handing down the heavy canvas sacks of coins to two men standing in a light wagon. One of the men held a double-barreled shotgun. Destined for the vault of the Wells, Fargo bank a few doors away, Ross guessed. The company had been the first bank in Virginia City, before they bought the Pioneer Stage Line and added the express business.

It felt good to stretch his legs as he walked down the street, looking for a restaurant open early. He needn't have worried. He'd half expected a deserted street at this hour, but every store and saloon was open; pedestrians streamed up and down the boardwalks, crossing the mud streets, stepping over or sloshing through puddles. The place was as busy as midday. Was it a weekend? He had to stop and think. After a few seconds, his tired brain figured out it was Thursday, May 3rd or 4th. Apparently Virginia City never closed down to sleep. Where were all these people going this time of day? Then he remembered the mines worked on two twelve-hour shifts. It didn't matter to miners if it were day or night when they were hundreds of feet underground.

He saw several workingmen's bars, but was looking for something other than pickled eggs and cheese that comprised the free lunch in such places. *Hennessy's Saloon* looked pretty good. A few doors away a sign announced *Chuvel's Restaurant.* He'd check that place later for a steak. In mid-block was *Barnam's Restaurant.* As soon as he walked in, his nose identified coffee and frying bacon, and he knew he'd made a good choice.

Ross pulled up a chair at a small table, dropped his bedroll and small handgrip.

A chunky, mustached waiter with a towel over one shoulder sauntered up. "What'll it be?" he asked.

"Bacon, scrambled eggs, fried potatoes . . . and plenty of coffee," Ross said without consulting a menu.

"You got it." The waiter turned up a heavy porcelain mug that was on the table. "Help yourself to the coffee from that urn over on the bar." He walked away toward the kitchen in the rear.

Ross went to the bar and drew a cup of hot coffee. He glanced at a bucket beside the urn that contained a small silver pitcher of cream resting in crushed ice. He looked again. Ice? For a frontier mining town, this place had all the amenities. But, ice? He was amazed to find cream cooling here in midsummer. He added cream to his coffee, stirred it with a spoon, and took a sip. *"Ahhh!"* Just what he needed after that night on the stage.

He turned back toward his table — and collided hard with someone. The steaming coffee sloshed down the front of the man's shirt and vest, and he jumped back.

"Aaggh! You clumsy bastard!"

"Sorry, mister. I didn't see you."

"Sorry, my ass!" He went into a crouch and yanked a sheath knife from his belt. "You scalded the hell outta me. Nobody does that and lives. I aim to cut your damned gizzard out!" Saliva trickled from the corner of his mouth and down his stubbled chin.

Ross felt his heart pounding, and he reached for his gun. But then hesitated. Judging from the unco-ordinated movements and bloodshot eyes, the man was drunk. He'd been standing at the bar when Ross came in. Ross backed away, taking his hand off the butt of his Colt. "I said I was sorry. I'll pay for your clothes, or to have your burns treated."

"Shit!" The man lunged forward, thrusting to eviscerate him. Ross dropped the mug and pivoted away like a bullfighter. He was vaguely aware of a commotion in the room as others jumped up to see the fight.

The attacker missed and staggered off balance.

Thunk! The man fell like a sack of sand, face down on the floor. Standing in front of Ross, a slim man was holstering a long-barreled pistol. "Somebody drag him outta here and douse him in the water trough."

Three patrons jumped to obey, grinning at the opportunity. One got him by the booted legs and two others under each arm and carried him out the front door. A hum of conversation resumed as the customers took their seats or turned back to the polished bar.

Ross regarded the man who'd buffaloed the drunk. "Much obliged. I could've handled that, but I didn't want to shoot a man who was obviously too drunk to fight. Besides, I don't think he even had a gun."

"He hocked it long ago for booze," the man said calmly. "Calvin Tibbs is a fixture here. Not a bad sort when he's sober . . . which ain't often." He reached past Ross and picked up another mug. "Here, fill up and join me, if you're of a mind to."

Ross obeyed and followed the man to his table.

"People get up mighty early in this town," Ross noted.

"Hell, most of them haven't been to bed.

In another hour, this place will be packed with miners coming off their shift at six."

Ross noted the man wore a stylish mustache and goatee, longish hair, a white shirt, and vest. The walnut butt of a pistol peeked out from beneath the vest. A black frock coat hung on the back of his chair. He regarded everything with the calm eyes of a man in familiar surroundings.

"Sorry I didn't introduce myself," the slim man said, offering his hand. "Name's Martin McNulty. But nobody around here calls me that. I'm known as the Sierra Scrivener, or just Martin Scrivener."

Ross arched his brows.

"That's my *nom de plume*. I've been the editor of *The Territorial Enterprise* since it came to town in 'Fifty-Nine."

"Gilbert Ross." He gripped the editor's hand. The handshake was firm. Ross then realized the black under McNulty's fingernails was printer's ink — not dirt or grease as he'd first assumed.

"A lot of people pass through this town every day, but I don't recall your face. And I pride myself on remembering faces."

"I just got off the stage from Placerville."

"Ah, the Wells, Fargo night run made it through all right, then."

"Mighty near didn't." He went on to

27

relate the details of the attempted robbery.

The editor quickly retrieved a pad and pencil from his vest pocket and began jotting notes. "For the next edition."

Just then the waiter arrived with a steaming plate of bacon, eggs, and potatoes.

"You got any hot sauce?"

The waiter brought a small bottle, and Ross dribbled a few drops on his eggs. "Too bland without something," he said when he saw Scrivener eyeing him.

"To each his own," the editor said, indicating his own food.

For the first time, Ross noted what Scrivener had before him — a big slice of lemon pie with meringue. He was washing it down with a foamy mug of beer. "Both tart," he explained. "They kinda go together. Mighty tasty breakfast after putting the paper to bed, and before I go home. They make the best pie here." He gestured over his shoulder. "My compositor and one of my reporters are back there having a few beers. Trent Billings and Sam Clemens. Both about twenty years younger than I am. They like to blow off steam after work. I long ago tired of all that. Don't have the stamina any more." He smiled and sipped his beer.

Ross had met many people in his travels. He trusted his instinctive assessment of individuals, and he liked this man.

"What brings you to Virginia City?"

Ross explained he was a mine inspector. "I was here briefly in 'Sixty, but we didn't cross paths. Things were pretty wild and woolly then."

"Still are, but in a different way."

"I could use your help directing me to a few of the mines. Have to make a detailed report on the mineral wealth of the region."

"Sure thing. Of course, you probably know about the Comstock and the Ophir, two of the biggest and richest. You figuring to invest yourself?" He regarded Ross with a steady gaze.

Ross shook his head while he finished chewing a strip of thick bacon. "The government couldn't have hired a better man for the job," he said. "I have no interest in that. Totally immune to gold fever and silver lust." He grinned.

"A man in a thousand," Scrivener remarked. He paused to attack the rest of his lemon pie.

"Where'd they get that ice?" Ross asked.

"Cut blocks out of the lakes in the mountains," he replied around a mouthful. "Pack it in sawdust in local ice houses. Usually lasts till late summer."

"And the cream?"

"Hell, since you were here four years ago, this town has everything that can be hauled over the mountains from San Francisco . . . Havana cigars, brandy, French champagne, oysters . . . anything and everything. A handful of millionaire mine owners have it all in their mansions. The rest of us have to make do with it in the saloons and clubs in town."

"Hmmm. . . ."

"John Mackay has a place you wouldn't believe . . . full of things like marble statuary, Flemish paintings, Waterford crystal, walnut and mahogany furniture. As befitting a silver nabob, his doorknobs, ashtrays, cuspidors, and plumbing fixtures are all made of silver. The upper crust have their own plush establishments here in town, and they and their wives travel to and from in liveried carriages. If money can buy it, they've got it. And it's new money. Most of those mine owners arrived here with one shirt and a pair of overalls. Fate smiles only on the favored ones."

Both men had finished their food and lounged back in their captain's chairs.

"If you've got time, I'd like to hire you to give me a tour," Ross said.

Scrivener was silent for several seconds. Finally he said: "You have any experience with that Navy Colt you're packing?"

"Some. But only in self-defense."

"Then I'll trade you. I'll take you on a thorough tour, if you'll watch my back for the next week or so."

Ross waited for an explanation.

"I got the editor of *The Gold Hill Clarion* all riled up. Mind you . . . I've had personal confrontations in the past . . . even been called out twice before . . . challenged to duels . . . when I was a young man in Mississippi. And I managed to survive." He paused. "But this man, Frank Fossett, is a no-good, lying, hoodwinking son-of-a-bitch, and I said so in print. He's bought worthless mines, salted 'em, and sold 'em to suckers." He never raised his soft voice as he denounced this enemy. "And I have it on good authority, he's screwing the wife of one of his employees. Now that I've exposed him, he's after my hide. And, knowing him, he won't have the guts to come at me *mano a mano.* Besides being a liar and a cheat, he has all the markings of a cowardly back-shooter."

Ross considered this proposal. He'd just hit town. Did he really want to become embroiled in someone else's trouble? His first impression of Scrivener was positive — a man of integrity and courage. And the man *had* disposed of the knife-wielding drunk with no hesitation.

"I'm no gun hand, but I'll do what I can," Ross said.

Scrivener seemed to relax. "Couldn't ask for any more than that."

CHAPTER THREE

Either Ross had quickly become used to the noise of Virginia City, or he was exhausted when he went to sleep. He didn't wake in his hotel bed until 4:00 p.m. From beneath his slightly open second-story window came the low rumble of street noise — voices, laughter, hoof beats slopping through mud, *squeaking* of ungreased wagon wheels, the wheezy chords from a music box in a nearby saloon, a steam whistle in the distance. Underlying all other sounds was the monotonous, never-ceasing *clanking* and *thumping* of the stamp mills.

After he'd left Martin Scrivener this morning, he'd gone down the street to a tonsorial parlor for a haircut and shave. Following that came a soak in a hot soapy tub of water at a Chinese bathhouse while his clothes were washed. By the time he reached the six-story, brick International Hotel, checked in, and gotten to sleep, it was 9:30 a.m.

He swung his feet to the floor, stood up, and stretched mightily, his muscles stiff and sore from rattling around in the stage all night. Splashing water from the pitcher into the bedside bowl, he doused his face, raking wet hands through his hair. Wiping his face on a towel, he glanced outside through the wavy glass. The sun, dulled by a haze of high cloud, rested atop nearby Mount Davidson. He had the strangest feeling he'd wasted the day in bed. Normally a daytime person, he was now rested and ready for work, but had nothing to do, and a long night stretched before him. It would be tomorrow before Martin Scrivener, as he called himself, would introduce him to the mine superintendents so he could begin making surveys of their operations.

As he buttoned his shirt, he smiled at his reflection in the mirror. Much of his data gathering could be done above ground from ore samples, records and statistics, and interviews with mine owners. But any written records could be exaggerated, if not purposely falsified. The contents of ledgers had to be verified by first-hand evidence when he descended hundreds of feet into torch-lit tunnels, talked to miners, and examined the diggings himself. The miners made good wages, but worked under trying conditions — dependent on topside blowers to force breathable air into the shafts and drifts, where poison gas, cave-ins, explosions, scalding, and flooding were ever-present dangers. The steamy heat was so debilitating in some areas, the shirtless miners worked only a half hour at a stretch before resting in an underground room supplied with ice and water.

He checked out of the International Hotel; the rates were too rich for his government salary. One day of luxury was all he allowed himself. Then it was back to reality. A block away on C Street he ensconced himself comfortably in the Algonquin, a two-story hostelry that was reasonably clean and apparently free of vermin. After he dumped his duffel and returned to the street to find an eatery for an early supper, he was struck again at the appearance of the town. It had taken on a look of permanence with many brick buildings replacing the wooden shanties that had been here four years earlier. Even the wooden stores and saloons seemed more substantial, interspersed with the taller brick and stone structures. He passed *Scholl & Roberts Gunsmiths, Young America Saloon, Light and Allman's Livery Stable.* It seemed nearly every other building was a saloon, and they never lacked for customers, any time of day or night. Wells, Fargo must be doing a healthy freighting business just to keep this town supplied with beer and liquor. He heard two gunshots, muffled by the walls of a building. No one on the street paused or even looked in that direction. Just part of the normal cacophony.

The two main streets of Virginia City ran fairly straight, paralleling the steep hills on the west. Evidently the town wasn't planned; it just happened, with everyone building wherever he could secure a lot. The result was a hodge-podge of buildings. Viewed from a high window or a hill, the shingle roofs looked like a dropped deck of cards. Many of the streets branched off at acute angles in search of open space. They apparently were not laid out, but rather followed the dips, spurs, and angles of the Comstock veins. There was nothing level about the town. The streets tilted up and down. Buildings on one side of the street were set against hillsides, their second or third stories at ground level in the rear.

Still, in late afternoon, the streets were blocked by immense freight wagons with ponderous wheels, heaped with mountainous loads of ore for the mills. Axles *squealed* and groaned with piles of merchandise in boxes, bales, bags, and crates. Eight to sixteen horses, mules, or oxen were required to haul each wagon. Even with the teamsters *cracking* their long whips and swearing mightily, the draft animals, sweating and steaming in the chill air, could barely drag their cargos up the slopes and through the deep ruts.

Ross found a café and had a sandwich and a beer for supper, then set off to find Martin Scrivener at the offices of *The Territorial Enterprise*. He had no problem following the editor's directions, and spotted the sign on the building from a half block away. The newspaper was located on the ground floor of a two-story brick building, tall windows looking out on the beehive city.

Ross walked in and saw two men with composing sticks setting type. Judging from the speed with which their fingers worked, they were very experienced, and didn't look up when he entered. The place had the peculiar smell of printer's ink, along with the faint aroma of cigar smoke.

Just then, Scrivener came out of his office in the rear of the room, a sheaf of copy in his hand. "Ah, Gil, glad to see you. Have a good day's sleep?" The editor looked as if he hadn't slept much. He slipped off his wire-rimmed glasses and dropped them into his vest pocket.

"Tolerable. Stayed at the International."

"High-toned lodgings."

"Had to move. My pocketbook couldn't stand it. I'm at the Algonquin now."

The editor nodded. "Not a bad place. But, if you'll be here a couple of weeks, I recommend my boarding house."

"Show me the way," Ross said. "Guess I just assumed you had a house here."

Scrivener guided him into his own office since the pressmen were making too much noise for conversation. "No. Thought about it," he said, gesturing for Ross to take a chair. "Virginia City was more than my wife could put up with . . . wide open, day and night, shootings, stabbings, me coming home from work about the time she was getting up." He shrugged. "Bought a little place for her and the daughter over in Sacramento. I take the stage over every chance I get . . . maybe once a month or so." Placing a lumpy paperweight of silver ore on his stack of papers, he smiled. "The arrangement seems to work," he said as if he had to further explain his domestic situation. "Fact is, I think maybe she was tired of me, rather than of all the constant hullabaloo in this mining town."

Ross thought it better not to comment.

"Oh, by the way," Scrivener said, putting on his glasses and locating two sheets of paper. He handed them across the desk. "Here's something for you to read. It's the account of your stage trip from Placerville last night. See if it comes close to what happened. If you told it to me accurately, it needs no embellishments."

At first glance, Ross thought the editor's desk a cluttered chaos. But all stacks and sheaves of papers and advertising handbills were carefully arranged in some sort of order. Scrivener's handwriting was neat and legible, although written with a dashing flair, as if the writer were enjoying himself. He quietly scanned the piece.

"Accurate to the last detail, and you've even dramatized it by shaping up my English when quoting me."

"I'm glad you approve because it's being set in type right now for tomorrow's edition. I got the jump on *The Gold Hill Clarion.*"

"That bit you added about me being here to survey and report on the mineral resources might help me get a foot in the door at some of the mines."

"No doubt."

"These people know and trust you."

He nodded. "Some of these mine owners

are close-mouthed about what they have or haven't discovered," Scrivener said, leaning back in his chair and looking over his spectacles. "Word always leaks out from the miners themselves if there's a new vein, or if they've broken through the face of a drift and hot water's flooding in. News like that can't be kept secret. But in that short interim of a day . . . or even a few hours before the shift changes . . . thousands of dollars in stock stand to be gained or lost, depending on who has the earliest inside information. So don't expect to be let in on anything new. The superintendents or foremen will show you what they want you to see."

"Fine. The daily fluctuations are not what I'm after, anyway. I want the long-term, general picture."

"I forgot, you're not here for your own financial gain or to speculate in hot stock." The editor smiled, giving the impression he really knew better.

"It actually bores me," Ross insisted. "If I owned a fistful of stock in the richest mine on the Comstock, I'd throw it in a drawer and probably forget where I put it."

"You're one of those who could go sound asleep in a raucous stockholders' meeting."

"That's about it. I have to be out in the

field doing something physical in order to take any interest, or get any satisfaction from a job. Fortunes won and lost on paper are not as exciting as reading a good adventure novel."

"You'll be in the field tomorrow. We'll take my buggy and drive down to Gold Hill and Silver City toward Carson. Unless you have a preference, we can start with the Crown Point on the divide between here and Gold Hill."

"Good enough."

Scrivener stood up and stretched, covering a yawn. "I'm going to make an early night of it. Be in bed by two."

"They won't be going home early?" Ross jerked a thumb toward the men working in the next room.

"Naw. My associate editor, Silas Bonner, will keep 'em at it till the paper's put to bed. Most of the younger men are single and like the night life. But. . . ." He paused. "I'd fire anyone who leaves without finishing." Then he grinned. "I also give them an added incentive to stay here and get the job done night after night. *The Enterprise* furnishes up to ten gallons of beer from Chauncey's Saloon next door."

"Ten gallons *per day?*"

Scrivener nodded. "Gets pretty hot and

dry in that composing room on summer nights. It also helps fire the imaginations of some of my reporters when they're writing up their articles. Makes for some very creative prose."

Ross whistled softly. "A lot of men I know would like to have a job with those fringe benefits."

"Helps make up for the marginal pay. Keeps some of the more wild-eyed ones from plunging over their heads into stocks, or quitting and going off prospecting themselves . . . especially now that all the good ore deposits are owned by big companies. No more surface placer mining where a man can sluice out the gravel and come up with anything more than a few grains of gold. The silver ore is hundreds of feet underground. Hard-rock miners make a better salary than my men, but it's tough, dangerous work, and they generally don't live as long."

The two men walked into the large room with the high ceiling. One of the men in an ink-stained apron came over to Scrivener, holding a wet proof sheet, and said something that Ross didn't catch. The editor glanced at the sheet.

"Don't rewrite the head. Reduce the type to make it fit," the editor said.

The man nodded, and moved away.

"I'll look for you in the morning," Ross said, reaching for the door handle. The twilight had deepened to dusk and C Street was lighted by the glow from several dozen stores and saloons.

Silhouetted against the lamplight of many businesses, a lone horseman came galloping down the street, weaving in and around the wagon and horse traffic. The rider held a flaming torch in one hand, wind whipping the flames over his shoulder.

Ross opened the door and stepped out onto the boardwalk. He heard *thrumming* hoofs just as the horse veered to his side of the street, nearly galloping up onto the sidewalk. Ross instinctively dived sideways. The rider's extended arm came up, flinging the blazing torch end over end. It crashed through one of the tall front windows of the newspaper office, and the interior of the room burst into flame.

Ross ducked flying particles of glass, then sprang into the street, yanking his Colt. Thumbing back the hammer, he brought up the weapon and held his breath. *Steady . . . don't hit anyone else,* he thought. Horse and rider were receding down the darkened street when Ross fired. The Navy Colt bucked and roared, a yellow tongue of flame darting from the long barrel. He fired again, and saw the rider reel in the saddle just before a bend in the street screened him from view.

"Somebody get the sheriff!" he yelled, holstering his gun and dashing back inside where the entire staff was fighting the fire. The torch had struck a container of type cleaner and the flames were licking up the wall.

"Fossett!" Scrivener hissed as he grabbed up a cuspidor and flung its contents on the blaze. One of the compositors had been splashed with the burning liquid and his co-workers were rolling him in a coat to smother the flames.

Ross snatched up a heavy container of sand near the door and, face averted from the heat, threw it at the base of the blaze near the wall. The flames instantly dropped, but the fire still burned. Thank God the inside of the wall was rough brick with no paneling or wallpaper.

A fire bell *clanged* somewhere outside, apparently summoning a volunteer fire company.

One of the men ran to the edge of the flames, kicking bales of paper out of the way. Another grabbed up two small buckets of beer and flung them on the burning wooden floor.

Ross stripped off his coat, doused it with beer, and began beating the edges of the spreading flames.

It was less than ten minutes, but it seemed like a stretch in purgatory before the *clanging* of an approaching bell signaled the arrival of the horse-drawn fire wagon. The volunteers had drilled themselves well and took over with no confusion or wasted motion. Two men grabbed the pump handles on each side of the tank while two others unreeled the hose and another secured the big draft horses. Within a minute, the brawny men had the hose spraying the fire through the broken front window. As they beat back the blaze, they advanced, stepping through the window frame, playing the stream of water at the base of the fire, then on nearby flammable furniture.

Within minutes, the blaze was out. The firemen continued to wet down the steaming wall and floor. The room was filled with smoke and steam, and a nauseating charred odor.

The newspaper workers had retreated out onto the sidewalk, coughing to clear their lungs of the smoke that continued to billow out the open door and the shattered window frame. A quick survey showed no one injured except the burned compositor. A crowd had quickly gathered and blocked the street around the fire engine, a buzz of conversation filling the air. Ross and Scrivener stood to one side, watching the efficient volunteer fire company work, making sure no embers remained to re-ignite.

"I told you Fossett wouldn't have the guts to challenge me to a duel," Scrivener said, wiping his sweaty face with a handkerchief, leaving a streak of soot on his cheek.

Ross took a deep breath of clean air. "You had him pegged. Low-down coward to torch a man's business, not caring who he might burn up in the process."

"And he thinks he got away with it, because I can't prove he did it."

"Don't know if he personally slung the torch, but I'm almost sure I wounded that rider."

Scrivener turned to him with a slow smile. "So maybe we *do* have proof . . . if we can find him."

Ross shook his head. "Unless it's Fossett himself, it'll be hard to say. Too many men shot in this town every day to make a wound anything unusual. And my Thirty-Six-caliber Navy lead ball is common enough. But we can get the law to investigate."

"What law?" the editor countered. "Like

the stock market, this place pretty much regulates itself. There's supposed to be a sheriff over in Carson City, but don't know that anybody sees much of him. The police force here is a joke."

Ross gestured at the damaged office. "Did he put you out of business?"

"Hell no! The press is OK. Looks like we saved the ink and there's still plenty of dry paper. It'd take more than that to keep *The Territorial Enterprise* from publishing."

Scrivener stepped up to a muscular, red-faced man who was supervising the fire-fighting effort. "Murph, I want to thank you and the boys for a helluva good job saving the paper."

"That's what we train for," the big man said, pulling off his gloves. "The way the wind's blowing tonight, the whole town could've gone up, if this'd gotten away from us. We'll stand by for a couple hours to make sure it's completely out."

The crowd in the street was beginning to disperse now that the excitement had died down.

"Let's get this place cleaned up, men," Scrivener said, stepping back inside the office. "We'll have that window boarded up tomorrow."

"I'll stay and help," Ross said.

Scrivener surveyed the damage, hands on hips. "How badly is Bill burned?"

Two men were gently removing the tattered remains of Bill's charred shirt. The injured man was flinching as the cloth adhered to the raw spots.

"Dunno yet."

Scrivener went into his office and jerked open a desk drawer. "Here, slather some of this on him and go get the doctor. You know where he lives? Roust him out of bed if you have to." He handed over a tin of *Mabrey's Analgesic Balm*.

The editor looked at the others who appeared to be in shock. "Somebody open that back door and let's get a cross draft in here to clear out some of this smoke. Break out the brooms." He turned to a curly-haired, mustached young man standing nearby. "Clemens, you have experience as a typesetter. Drop whatever you're working on and jump in there and take Bill's place for now. First, check that case and see how much of the lead type was melted." To his young assistant editor he barked: "Kill the lead story. I'm writing a new one. Banner head." He stepped inside his office and snatched a pad off the desk, pulled a pencil from his pocket, and slipped on his glasses.

Ross watched over his shoulder as he

wrote in block letters: *ENTERPRISE AT-TACKED.* Beneath that, in smaller letters: *Cowardly Enemy Torches Newspaper Office.* Farther down, in normal cursive, he wrote: *Attacker Wounded And Will Be Apprehended Soon.* He pulled out his desk chair and sat down, finishing the article quickly.

"You going to accuse Fossett in print?" Ross asked.

Without looking up, Scrivener replied: "Not using his name, but I'm leaving no doubt I know who did it, and why. For anyone who reads this, it won't be hard to guess."

"Don't want to tell you your business, but aren't you adding fuel to the fire? Maybe we should wait and see if we can find that wounded man first."

Scrivener looked up. "You'd never make it in the newspaper business. This is the kind of thing that sells papers. And I'm not letting that coward off the hook for a minute."

Ross shrugged. "Suit yourself." He grabbed a push broom standing against the wall and began sweeping shattered glass and blackened water toward the open front door.

Scrivener finished, scanned the piece, and handed it to Sam Clemens. "You and Baxter start setting that."

"Your men didn't panic," Ross said when

Scrivener came to stand beside him near the front door. "And they did a great job keeping that fire under control until the firemen got here."

"I might increase their beer ration," Scrivener said under his breath.

"For morale, or to put out fires?"

"Both. They can drink it for morale, and run it through to put out any fires."

CHAPTER FOUR

It was nearly noon the next day before Martin Scrivener and Gil Ross rolled south out of town in the editor's buggy.

"By God, all of Washoe will know about Fossett's attack," Scrivener said, snapping the reins on the back of the sorrel, urging him to a trot.

"Guess I'll really have to watch your back now," Ross said, yawning and stretching. He'd been in town less than thirty-two hours but it felt more like a week.

"That sneaky, torch-throwing s.o.b. slowed us down. The morning edition hit the streets two hours late."

Ross wondered if all editors took this much pride in their jobs. If he worked at a newspaper, it'd have to be an evening publication; he couldn't stand to work all night and sleep all day. In spite of Scrivener's resolve to make an early night of it, neither man had departed the damaged *En-*

terprise office until nearly 5:00 a.m. The editor had left two men on guard to be sure the fire-throwing attacker or someone else didn't come back to finish the job. Ross thought a twenty-four-hour guard would have to be posted to prevent any further destruction. Scrivener was on the defensive now. Ross had heard of these battles between editors before, and had assumed they were all contrived to keep up interest and circulation in both papers. He was convinced that wasn't the case here.

The wind was light out of the southwest today, making for a beautiful, warm spring day. He settled back to enjoy the ride.

"As long as we're running this far behind in our schedule," Scrivener said, "I thought we'd shoot on down to Carson City and leave word at the sheriff's office . . . for whatever good that'll do. On the way back, you can take a look at the mines and decide where you want to go later."

"Good idea. I didn't see much the other morning from the stage. It was barely daylight and I was tired."

Shortly after, as they drove up the saddle that divided Virginia City from Gold Hill, Scrivener pointed. "There's the Crown King. We'll catch it on the way back."

"A big operation," Ross said, noting the

hoisting works, the big buildings, the smoke billowing from a tall stack.

"Not the largest, by any means," the editor said.

By 2:00 p.m. they'd reached Carson City and left a report of the fiery raid with the sheriff's office. As expected, the lawman was not there, and the deputy, sunning himself on the porch, could hardly be stirred to take down the details.

"That report's probably already in the files . . . or the stove," Scrivener said as he guided his sorrel back the way they'd come.

"I hear tell there's to be a branch mint in Carson to avoid having to freight all that bullion over the Sierras to the San Francisco mint," Ross said.

"There's some movement in that direction. A fella bought some land and is petitioning Congress to authorize and fund it."

"Sounds like a good idea to me," Ross said. "The sooner, the better. That would save a lot of money and prevent a lot of robberies."

The editor nodded. "It'll be built about the time the last glacier melts in Alaska."

"A bit pessimistic."

"The usual political wrangling. Some for, some against. Everyone has a selfish motive. Of course, there's a war on and Congress doesn't want to fund anything they don't have to."

"But a mint would be to the government's advantage. More specie in circulation."

"I know. Maybe they're waiting until Nevada is admitted to the Union. I think it'll eventually happen as long as the mines here are producing. But I'm not holding my breath waiting to spend the first coins it mints."

Ross looked ahead, thinking he'd prepared himself for the changes between Carson City and Virginia City. But he was overwhelmed by what he saw. "Is this Empire City?"

"Yep."

"This used to be sagebrush, inhabited by an old man named Dutch Nick. Just look at it now."

The valley along the head of the Carson River was filled with quartz mills and sawmills. The hammering of stamps, the *hissing* of steam, the whirling clouds of smoke from tall chimneys, and confused clamor of voices from crowds of workmen reminded him of some manufacturing city in the East.

A bit farther beyond, at Silver City, was more of the same. From the descent into the cañon through the Devil's Gate, and up the grade to Gold Hill, stretched a nearly continuous line of mills, dumps, sluices, water wheels, frame shanties, and grog shops. Gold Hill had swelled to the size of a small city, and was now a continuation of Virginia City. The whole hill was riddled and honeycombed with shafts and tunnels, some apparently abandoned. Engine houses for hoisting were perched on points that appeared nearly inaccessible. Quartz mills of various sizes lined the side of the cañon. The main street was flanked by brick stores, hotels, express offices, saloons, and restaurants.

"Shall we stop in Gold Hill and see if Fossett is at the *Clarion* office?" Ross suggested, only half in jest. "He's liable to be home nursing that wound I gave him. Who knows? It could be serious."

Scrivener grunted. "If I see him, I'll probably finish him off." He flipped a latch and pushed back the top of the buggy so the afternoon sun shone fully on them.

"That feels good," Ross said. He was in his shirt sleeves since his coat had been ruined the night before when he'd soaked it in beer and used it to help beat out the fire.

"I used to rattle around this camp in a buckboard, but finally decided, when I hit fifty, that I'd had enough of the elements.

Invested in a buggy with a folding top and some leaf springs. The comforts of middle age."

If the editor was getting soft, it wasn't apparent to Ross.

They rode in silence for a few minutes while Ross surveyed more of the large and small mining operations that covered nearly every square yard of the mountainsides. Dozens of swarthy, bearded, dust-covered men were piercing the grim mountains, ripping them open, thrusting murderous holes through their crusty bodies, setting up engines to cut out their vital arteries, stamping and crushing up their disemboweled fragments, and holding fiendish revels amid the chaos of destruction. Their numbers and ruthless energy reminded him of nothing so much as swarms of termites on huge earthen mounds he'd seen on a Caribbean island. But the earth was fighting back, as if it had a vengeful mind against its human tormentors. The mighty mountains rose up to strike down these puny men with disease and death. *Do your worst,* it seemed to say. *Dig, delve, pierce, and bore with your picks and shovels and machines to wring out a few drops of my precious blood. Hoard it, spend it, gamble for it, damn your souls for it. You rip and rave, but you are finite. Do what you will, but I will win out in the end. Sooner or later, death will strike you down and I'll swallow your remains. From dust you came and to dust you will inevitably return. The earth alone endures.*

"Gil! Gil!"

Scrivener's voice cut into his deep reverie.

"Huh? Oh, sorry . . . what did you say?"

"Here we are."

Ross looked up to see they were stopped in front of the tin-sided building housing the hoisting works of the Crown King Mine. Inside, they found a muscular man in overalls and wool shirt inspecting a frayed cable. Scrivener introduced Ross to Jacob Krug, the foreman. Ross's hand was enveloped and nearly crushed by the man's grip.

"A mine inspector, is it? And you want to take a look down below?" The burly man stood with legs apart and hands on hips as he looked Ross up and down. "We inspect our own mine every day. We don't need any government man to do it for us."

Ross was instantly irritated, but patiently explained: "I'm only reporting a general idea of the potential of the minerals in Washoe so the government will have an idea of what it's worth when statehood comes."

"You can write in your report that the Crown King is doing as well as can be expected, what with all the competition around here."

Ross shrugged. "There are plenty of other mines I can examine. They'll be mentioned by name and I'm sure their stock will increase as a result of my published report."

Krug seemed to deflate slightly. "We ain't got nothing to hide, mind you. It's just that we got miners down there working, and we can't be responsible for any visitors. Could be dangerous, you know."

"Quite all right, Mister Krug," Ross said, climbing back into the buggy. Scrivener slapped the reins over the sorrel and they rolled away.

"Where to?" Scrivener inquired.

"It's getting late in the day. Back to Virginia City. I've decided to check out of my hotel and move into your boarding house."

"For this area, you can't beat it. Nice and clean and quiet, away from all the ruckus of town. Widow lady runs it and charges twelve dollars a week, without board."

"Better than the two dollars a night I'm paying now."

"Tell you what . . . maybe you should cut your teeth on the Ophir Mine. It's one of the biggest and best run operations on the Comstock, and the foreman, Michael Flannery, is a good friend of mine. We'll go up there in the morning. Of course, there are any number of operations you'll probably want to delve into while you're here . . . the Consolidated Virginia close by the Ophir, the Belcher Mine, the Gould and Curry, Hale and Norcross, the Savage, the Yellow Jacket, and a few of the smaller ones, like the Lady Washington and the Trench. There are at least two dozen more. You can take your pick."

Ross nodded.

"On the way back, there's a nearby place in the desert I'd like to stop," Scrivener said. "I've picked up a few artifacts from ancient Indians . . . shards of pottery, and that sort of thing."

"Fine. Then we can eat supper. Somehow, lunch got away from us."

A few minutes later Scrivener reined up in a barren, deserted stretch of desert. He tied his horse to a splinter of rock. Ross stepped down, glad to stretch his legs and breathe fresh air, since they were on the windward side of the smoke stacks.

Scrivener walked along, studying the rocky ground. "At this time of day, when the sun's at a low angle, it's easier to spot anything on the ground that's not natural, something man-made."

To Ross, it looked just like any other patch of desert terrain with almost no plants. The poisonous fall-out from the smoke stacks in the area had killed all the vegetation — no piñon, no juniper, no sage.

"Apparently, bighorn sheep lived in this region in centuries past. The ancient ones hunted them, along with pronghorn antelope and mule deer. Evidence indicates there must have been a decent growth of wheat grass, needle grass, buckwheat, rice grass, and rabbitbrush." He squatted and moved his head from side to side, carefully scanning the rocky ground, then rose, moved a few more yards, and repeated the process.

Of all the hobbies a man like Martin Scrivener might have, hunting ancient artifacts was one that seemed completely at odds with his normal life. But that's exactly why it made sense — a relaxing escape from the pressure of his job as editor of *The Territorial Enterprise.*

"Ahh!" Scrivener sprang forward and picked up a tiny stone. "Look!" He held out an arrowhead. "An Elko corner-notched projectile point . . . probably from a hunting spear, by the size of it."

"Your really know your points."

The editor smiled. "Been a passion of

60

mine since I was a kid. This one is a rare beauty. Not even damaged. Made and used between One Thousand B.C. and Five Hundred A.D." He rubbed the dirt from it. "Just think . . . this point probably brought down game, more than once, during a period when the Greek or the Roman civilizations dominated the known world. Those Mediterranean empires had no idea North America or its inhabitants even existed. Even though they might be broken, every spear point or arrowhead that was ever made is still in existence . . . somewhere. It just takes a little patience to find them. I like to scout this area shortly after a good rain like we had the other night. It tends to wash them out if they've been covered up over time." He carefully wrapped the point in his handkerchief and put it in his jacket pocket. "I'm buying supper to celebrate," Scrivener said as they climbed back into the buggy. "This is the most exciting find I've made in a long time. Remind me to show you my collection."

They decided to eat at nearby Gold Hill, unhitching the sorrel and leaving him at the livery for water and grain. A leisurely, two-hour meal followed, with good conversation and good beer. When they finally walked out toward the livery stable, full darkness had fallen and the moon had not yet made an appearance.

Ross felt the bite of the night chill since he had no coat. He walked along, hands in pockets, shivering, when a sharp command burst out of the darkness.

"Throw up your hands!"

Ross felt the muzzle of a gun in his ribs. He brought his hands out of his pockets and put them over his head, the three double eagles from his right front pocket clutched tightly in his raised right hand.

Scrivener silently put up his hands as well.

The masked robber ordered them to turn their pockets inside out and empty everything into a sack he held. His total take was two pocket combs, two billfolds, three silver dollars, several pennies and dimes, a pad and pencil, and a handkerchief. The footpad stuffed the money into his pocket and apparently felt the spear point in the handkerchief. "What's this? A piece of ore? Some rich specimen, I'll wager. Where'd you get it?"

"No. It's an arrowhead. I collect Indian arrowheads."

"Shit!" The robber flung it down. "A few dollars worth of change. If you two ever come through here again without some money in your pockets, I'll blast you." He snorted in disgust, dumped their billfolds, combs, and other items on the ground, and faded away into the darkness.

Ross let out a deep breath and put the three $20 gold pieces back into his pocket. "Glad it was too dark for him to notice I had my fists balled up."

"The divide between here and Virginia City is a favorite place for robberies of men afoot at night." Scrivener was on his hands and knees to retrieve his spear point. "So many hold-ups, I don't even hear about them all, so I just have to generalize in the paper. Boring and repetitive."

"Probably not to the victims."

The men came out into the welcome light of storefronts as they neared the livery.

"Next time I come through here after dark, I'll be in a buggy or on a horse with my gun in hand," Ross vowed.

"You know . . . that man's voice sounded somehow familiar," Ross said, scratching his chin. But the name and face kept sliding off the edge of his consciousness and would not come into focus. "Maybe it'll come to me later."

CHAPTER FIVE

Next morning Ross stood at the Ophir Mine and watched Scrivener's buggy roll away.

"Here, put this on to keep your clothes clean," said Michael Flannery, the foreman, handing him a pair of well-used canvas coveralls coated with smears of clay and dirt, stiffened with the drippings of candle wax and whitewash.

Flannery was a wiry, black-haired son of Erin with sharp eyes that seemed to take in everything. The foreman led him up a small hill to the mouth of a narrow shaft, handed him a thick candle, and lit it. "Hold this so the light reflects from the palm of your hand," he said. "I'll go down first."

They backed into the opening and began descending a slightly canted ladder. The small opening and the sight of sky receded above them. The smoky wicks of their candles cast wavering light on the rough walls of the shaft. At the end of the ladder was a small spot of ground to stand on, similar to a landing. Then they started down another ladder. At the end of that one came another, and yet another, until Ross lost track of how many they'd descended. A large pipe descended parallel to the shaft. A ponderous pump somewhere was hoisting water from the depths of the mine.

Ross stepped down carefully, looking around him. It wasn't light enough to see if silver ore lay in the loose dirt or rock of the narrow shaft.

Every few steps, Flannery paused and held his candle near the dripping rocks and banks of earth. "There . . . you see it? Horblendic, feldspathic . . . graniferous! There . . . and there! See? Look at that forty-five degree dip. Very rich."

"Yes, I see." Ross ducked under a wooden beam and an overhanging spur of rock. He twisted himself around corners and stubbed his toe on piles of ore heaped on landings as they moved down from one level to the next.

Finally they reached the bottom. The square-set timbering was an ingenious invention of a German immigrant; it allowed men to burrow more than a thousand feet into the earth. Timbers eighteen inches square interlocked with one another to form hollow cubes of any desired size, like small rooms.

"Make way, gents. Stand aside!" came a call from ahead in the tunnel. Miners were pushing ore-filled handcars along the tracks. The whole tunnel wasn't over five feet wide. The tracks and cars took up three feet of that, the square-set timbers the rest. Ross and the foreman hugged a dark, wet wall as the ore cars rumbled past.

With Flannery leading the way, they explored the fifth level, and the sixth level. The foreman seemed in a hurry to rush him through for a cursory tour.

"Slow down," Ross said, crouching by a ledge of rock. "I want to take a closer look." He pulled the small, prospector's hammer from his belt and chipped off a sample.

At one point, miners were pitching down loose earth and rocks to the next level to be hauled out by ore cars. Ross and the foreman climbed up a long ladder.

When they'd reached the relative safety of the upper level, Flannery turned to Ross. "Recently two miners were killed by a dog in the main shaft."

"A dog?" He had visions of a wild, rabid dog loose in the tunnels.

"They were on their way up in a bucket. A dog tripped trying to run across the mouth of the shaft up top. Fell into the shaft and hit the men a hundred feet below, and down they all went another hundred and seventy-five feet to the bottom. Wasn't much left of them."

Flannery was apparently trying to throw a scare into an outsider. He didn't know Ross had crawled through many mines more dangerous than this one.

"That's about it," the foreman said, "unless there's something else you want to see. All these tunnels and shafts look about the same."

"I'm ready to go. Maybe I can jot down a few figures on your production, number of miners employed, how many miles of tunnels you have, capital outlay on equipment . . . that sort of thing."

"Sure." Flannery pointed the way they'd come down. "We can climb back up the ladders, or be dragged up the incline by a steam engine, or be hoisted up a shaft in a wooden bucket by means of a hand winch. Your choice."

Ross didn't relish the long, weary climb up a series of steep ladders. "I'll take the hand windlass," he said, choosing the least strenuous way.

He dispensed with the bucket and put a foot into a loop of the dangling rope. At a bell signal from the foreman, someone at the top began to hoist Ross. He bobbed around, swinging freely and scraped against the walls of the shaft. Eventually he arrived at the top and stepped off onto the landing platform.

Flannery gave him the statistics he asked for. Ross returned the coveralls and candle, then hiked back into town.

The usual crowds milled around the streets, sidewalks, saloons, and shops. The place hummed like a hornet's nest. Ross gazed in wonder at the handbills plastered and nailed to every square foot of space on store fronts, porch posts, fences, and walls. *Cheaper than running ads in the paper,* he thought. The bills were pushing everything — brandy, cigars, stomach bitters, cheap suits, the variety show at Maguire's Opera House. Under a boardwalk awning, an organ grinder was cranking out a melody on a well-used, one-legged music box, while a red monkey, less than two feet tall, scampered around at the end of a ten-foot tether, importuning all passers-by with his tin cup. Snatching out the coins that *clunked* into the cup, he handed them to his master.

Ross paused for a moment to watch.

"Now, where, outside of the Mediterranean, could a man see a sight like that?" a voice at his shoulder said.

Ross turned. "Sam Clemens."

"Actually you wouldn't see that sight in the Mediterranean at all," Clemens went on, "because that's a Red Uakari monkey. It's found in Peru and Brazil."

"Now, how in hell would you know that?"

Clemens shrugged. "I asked him."

"The man or the monkey?"

Clemens chuckled.

"I saw you at the *Enterprise* fire the other night, but we haven't been officially introduced. I'm Gilbert Ross, mine inspector and student of human nature."

"Now, there's a course you'll never graduate from," Clemens said, gripping his hand.

"Can I buy you a drink?" Ross asked.

"Sun's not quite over the yardarm yet," the curly-haired newsman replied. "Besides, I probably had more than my share last night. I'm just getting up and around, and was thinking of breakfast . . . or lunch."

"So was I. Fancy some company?"

"Sure. This looks as good as any."

They ducked into the nearby Howling Wilderness Saloon. A sign on the outside wall advertised a good square meal for 50¢.

Ross noticed the young reporter was looking a little rumpled — unshaven around the

69

heavy reddish mustache that hid his mouth, white shirt wrinkled, thick, curly hair appearing to have been combed with his fingers.

"Lunch is on me," Ross said. "I'm sixty dollars richer than I should be after a run-in with one of your hold-up men last night between here and Gold Hill." He related the incident of holding up his hands, clutching the gold coins.

"By God, I'd write up a short piece about that, but I'm afraid it'd just alert the next robber to the trick."

"Where you from, Sam?"

"Missouri. Been at the paper sixteen months. Couldn't seem to make a living mining."

"What made you come West?"

To Ross, the young man appeared to be on the underside of thirty.

"The war shut down commercial river traffic on the Mississippi, and ended my job piloting. Then my brother Orion was given a political appointment as secretary of the territorial government, and I came along as his unpaid assistant." He paused and proffered a cigar. Ross declined with a shake of his head. Clemens lighted one himself, his head disappearing behind a cloud of white smoke.

"Whew!" Ross fanned the air. "What *is* that?"

"A Wheeling long nine," Clemens replied, holding the cigar between thumb and forefinger and looking fondly at it. "Got acquainted with them when I was a cub pilot on the river. They have one virtue which recommends them above all other cigars."

"What's that?"

"They're cheap."

"I see," Ross said, sliding his chair back into clearer air.

"They're also deadly up to thirty paces."

"That's for sure. Probably kept away all the mosquitoes on the river, too."

"You bet." He took another puff and squinted at Ross through swirling smoke. "What's your story?"

Ross shrugged. "Been around the world, and wrote a few travel books. Studied geology. Served a spell as a correspondent for *Harper's Weekly.* Widower now. Grown kids. Presently working for the government as a mine inspector."

"Ever take a flyer in mining stock yourself?"

Ross shook his head. "Too much of a gamble for me, even if the stock is good when you buy it. Mother Nature is inconsistent with her gifts. I do keep my eyes open for certain friends and give them tips on good-looking mines."

"When I first came out here, I tried staking a claim and digging up the silver and gold myself. Found out that's more work than working, and damned little to show for it. Sold out for a tuppence and went to trading stock. Easier than working a shovel, but a lot riskier. Got fleeced. Finally took a job with the paper for wages, and went back to eating regular," he finished in a barely discernible drawl. His eyes twinkled with good humor as he puffed on his cigar. "Why, just last night I was offered a hundred running feet of the Scandalous Wretch at a dollar a foot. Not an hour later another friend tried to unload his two thousand shares of Bobtail Horse and Root Hog or Die for only ten cents a share."

"Oh?"

"They swore these were all producing mines over near Devil's Gate."

"Did you bite?"

"If I'd been a newcomer, I might've been tempted. As it was, I knew all three of those mines. They don't produce enough to pay the assessment. Pick and shovel operations, in spite of the fancy printing on the stock certificates. If they ever squeeze out as much as fifty cents' worth of silver to the acre, then I'm the next governor." He chuckled and signaled the waiter across the crowded room, then turned back to Ross. "Mind if I ask whether you're a single-ledge man or a multiple-ledge man?" He looked at Ross with narrowed eyes through the curling cigar smoke like a Pharisee about to trap Jesus with a loaded question.

But Ross was ahead of him. "I'm not quite the tenderfoot you take me for, Sam. If I say all the mines around here are but individual parts of a single ledge of rich ore, you'll report it in the paper and I'll be run out of town. The livelihood of every store-keeper, lawyer, and small mine owner depends on there being many ledges that underlie each other, criss-cross and go here, there, and yon in multiple directions."

Clemens laughed aloud. "You're not a geologist, then?"

"Closest thing to it. But even professors of geology or mining engineers have no way of knowing. Not even a man with a degree in geology could have the expertise to know whether it's one ledge or many, since the whole thing is buried hundreds of feet in the earth and protrudes through the surface only here and there. When I was here in Eighteen Sixty, when this place had just started to boom, I drew a map of what I thought the ledges looked like and where they ran. It resembled a handful of straw somebody'd thrown down on a board and varnished in place. But some fools took it for gospel, instead of my educated guess. Regardless of what I may think, personally I'm a multiple-ledges man in public." He pushed back his chair and crossed his legs, as the waiter arrived to take their order. They settled on the special — pork and beans, onions, cabbage, bacon, and sour-dough bread.

"The multiple-ledges theory is what keeps legions of lawyers in business," Clemens continued. "Nearly everybody on the Comstock is at dagger points in some kind of litigation over intersecting claims, and which ones have the right to follow which veins, and so on and on."

Ross nodded. "The lawyers are apparently the ones making all the real money in this town."

"The lawyers and the outlaws," Clemens added. "Or did I just repeat myself?"

"Are the legal judgments fair?"

"When a learned decision is handed down against a claimant, that's usually not the end of it. The case is then settled out of court as often as not. The loser shoots the winner."

"Then why don't they eliminate the middle man and go to gun play right off?"

"The territory would never become a state if its citizens ignored the law."

"So the judges' rulings are basically fair, but not respected?"

"We've got the most upright judges in the country down at Carson City. They're only considered corrupt if they take bribes from both sides at the same time."

"Couldn't ask for anything fairer than that," Ross said, suppressing a grin. "Are you working on a story today?"

"Sure am. Nothing big, but at least I don't have to invent something. A widow woman who lives a half mile from our cabin knocked the bottom out of her well."

"Sounds like the beginning of a tall tale."

"For once it's not. I walked over there to check it myself. Her well's about thirty feet deep. She went out and dropped a wooden bucket down to get some water. Bucket hit the water, and it was like somebody pulled a plug. The next minute, she had a bucket dangling on a rope with nothing below it. Turns out the Mexican Hat Mine workers, without knowing it, had tunneled right under her well. The water had gradually soaked through the thin layer of soil separating them. When she dropped the bucket, the concussion of it hitting the water broke right through into the tunnel."

"Only on the Comstock. . . ."

"I expect the whole town to collapse and slide down into the mines in the next few years."

"The robbers will have the place cleaned out by then," Ross said. "Does Virginia City have a police force?"

"The territorial government provides for one. But, as you can see, a handful of policemen have all the chance of chipmunks in a forest fire. Reckon that's why every man in town carries a gun to settle his own disputes." He frowned. "In my case, that may not be such a good idea."

"Why's that?"

"I'm the one mainly responsible for Martin Scrivener's getting into it with Frank Fossett, editor of *The Gold Hill Clarion.*"

"You?"

Clemens nodded. "I wrote two or three pieces about Fossett and repeated some rumors I'd heard about his low-down shenanigans of salting mines, and adultery, and possibly being the brains behind some stage hold-ups. Thought it'd be fun to hear him howl and call us a few names in print. Turned out most of my jabs hit a sore spot. Fossett didn't deny what I'd written. Guess he figured I had some kind of proof to back up what I said. He blew up and threatened Martin, thinking he was the one who'd exposed him."

"Why didn't he go after you?"

"My pieces didn't have a byline."

"I see."

"I started this while Martin was out of town for a week. Thought it might boost circulation." He shook his head. "It did more than that. Martin came back and heard all the ruckus. When he realized Fossett really was the whited sepulcher I'd made him out to be, Martin backed me with some editorials of his own. So, now Fossett's after *him.* But I can't stand by and let that happen. Martin Scrivener's too good a man to finish something I started."

"What can you do about it?"

Clemens didn't answer while the waiter set their food on the table.

"As you know, Fossett or one of his men tried to burn down the *Enterprise,*" Clemens continued. "I have to stop him before he does something even more desperate. The only thing I can think to do is own up to writing those pieces, and challenge him to a duel."

"Isn't there a law against dueling in this territory?"

"Yep. The law would have to clamp down on any crime as public as that. We'd both be arrested and jailed."

"You wouldn't have to advertise the time and place," Ross said.

"Quit trying to get me killed," Clemens said. "You don't think I actually *want* to fight a duel with deadly weapons, do you? I'd have to leak it to the press or put out a few broadsides with Fossett's name on them. Weak as they are, the police will have to be given a chance to prevent it." He spooned up a bite of pork and beans. "I may carry this six-shot Navy Colt, but if I were to fire it at the bartender over there, I'd just as likely fetch the bouncer by the door."

"Not a marksman, then?"

Clemens shook his head. "Especially when my nerves are playing hobs with my gun hand."

Ross wiped up some juice with a crust of bread and chewed thoughtfully.

"You don't want to go to jail, either. Why don't you have Fossett arrested for various and sundry crimes?"

"I have no proof."

"You're in a bind."

"To take Fossett's mind off Scrivener, I'll own up to the accusations, challenge him to a duel, and then make myself scarce for a while until things settle down."

"That won't do much for your reputation."

"As the Bible says . . . 'better a live mouse than a dead lion' . . . or something to that effect."

"I wouldn't be in your shoes for a controlling interest in the Comstock."

CHAPTER SIX

After lunch they parted, Clemens heading for the newspaper office and Ross starting up the street to find a men's clothing store, or a likely-looking mercantile to replace the coat he'd ruined. A half block ahead, seated on the edge of the boardwalk and leaning against a post, was a drunk — or a beggar. Ross slowed his pace for a look. Although beggars were few in this town, drunks were as common as hoof prints. What differed about this one was the hand-lettered sign he held propped in his lap. It read:

AVERY TUTTLE,
Owner of the Blue Hole Mine
A Robber, Liar, Murderer
Takes silver for the lives of miners

Most pedestrians walked around the man's legs sprawled out in the sidewalk. Others gave him only a curious glance as they passed. One or two stopped to read the sign as Ross came up. The man was emaciated, obviously drunk or sick, with a week's worth of whiskers, his eyes wearing a watery, glazed look that focused on nothing. As Ross watched, the man pulled a bottle from behind the sign and took a swig. From a few feet away, the square-faced bottle and label looked like some kind of patent medicine.

Ross was curious. If there was something about the Blue Hole Mine he should know, he meant to find out what it was. He hunkered down. "Hey mister, what's this about Avery Tuttle and his mine?"

The man turned in his direction and attempted to focus. His effort was interrupted by a sudden spasm of dry coughing. He finally stopped, and took a deep breath, but seemed even weaker than before.

"What about the Blue Hole?" Ross repeated.

"It'll kill ya," the man replied, struggling for enough breath to speak.

"Poison gas in the mine? No canaries there to warn you?" Ross prompted.

"No masks, no air, just rock dust," the man gasped.

"How about if I buy you something to eat?" Ross said. "You hungry?"

The man nodded weakly.

Ross took him around the shoulders and under the arms and helped him up. The stoppered bottle *clattered* to the boards. Ross put it in his pocket.

"My sign. . . ." The man reached back and clutched it as Ross aided him to the door of the first saloon he saw. Just inside, the man sagged into a chair at an empty table. Ross sat next to him, propping the sign against the wall.

"This here is one o' them two-bit saloons," the man objected.

"No matter. I'm paying," Ross said.

The so-called two-bit saloons were on the uphill side of the street and fancied themselves as higher class than the one-bit saloons below. They sported fancier fixtures, mirrors, better selection of liquors and wines, and a varied menu. Not only did they charge two bits a drink, but everything else was proportionally higher, from cigars to steaks. As a practical matter, a man couldn't pay just 12 1/2¢ for a drink in the lower-priced saloons since 1/2¢ coppers had long since gone out of circulation, so bartenders habitually returned as change for a quarter only a 10¢ piece or two silver half-dimes, making them one-bit saloons in name only.

Ross ordered the man a bowl of beef stew and a pint of beer.

"What's your name, mister?" Ross asked when the waiter had gone.

"Jacob Sturm," the man replied, trying to focus. His breath reeked of alcohol. Ross pulled out the half full, square-faced bottle and gently shook it, watching the deep amber contents swirl inside the clear glass. He read the yellow label. *Madam Turney's Mountain Elixir* was printed in flowing, ornate script across the top. In smaller lettering below, it professed to be a cure for corns, erysipelas, as well as dyspepsia, the grippe, flatulent colic, and botts. It prevented liver and heart ailments, and would relieve symptoms of mountain fever, colds, congestion, asthma, and shortness of breath. But Ross almost laughed aloud when he read the last line. *For botts, it has no equal.*

"That's m' medicine . . . for my lungs," Sturm said breathlessly.

Ross twisted out the cork and took a tentative sniff. "Holy shit!" He jerked back, eyes watering. "Guaranteed to cure or kill," he agreed.

"Makes me feel better," Sturm muttered.

"I can believe that." Ross corked the bottle and set it on the table. This Sturm was stronger than he appeared if he could swig Madam Turney's Elixir and stay upright.

"What's this about the Blue Hole Mine?"

Ross again asked.

"Avery Tuttle . . . a cruel man."

"He's the owner?"

"Yeah. Rock dust and gas ate up my lungs working at the Blue Hole."

"All the mines are dangerous like that."

Sturm shook his head. "Tuttle cuts corners. Men killed when rotten ropes break on the hoist. Foreman orders miners into drifts . . . where they're scalded by hot steam. Forces us to work in spaces where gas is leaking . . ." — he paused to gasp for breath — "beyond the reach of air blowers."

The waiter arrived with the stew and beer, took a silver dollar from Ross, and left.

Sturm was convulsed with a dry, hacking cough before he could begin eating. "I'm a walking dead man," he whispered as he took up his spoon.

For several seconds Ross was silent. Mine owners, in general, were not humanitarians. They would pay the cheapest wage they could, work the men as hard as possible, cut their overhead to a minimum, rake in big profits, and undercut or steal their neighbor's rich vein of ore if they got half a chance. Power, greed, and wealth brought out the worst in human nature. Yet, there were exceptions. He'd heard the Irish immigrant, John Mackay, one of the richest men on the Comstock, was the antithesis of most others in his honesty, integrity, and care for friends and employees. He was liked and admired by nearly everyone — a notable quality among the newly wealthy mine owners who'd come up from nothing. The miners had organized into a strong union to protect themselves from men like Avery Tuttle.

"You a union member?"

"Yeah."

"Didn't the union threaten to strike if the miners weren't paid four dollars a day?"

"That's right," Sturm said, looking up with bleary eyes. "And we got it, too."

"Seems like that kind of money would help make up for the bad working conditions."

Sturm looked at him suspiciously. "You part of management?"

"No. Just interested in your story. Go on."

"We took to tying bandannas over nose and mouth to filter the air. But it was too damned hot down there to keep those things on very long. Heat one hundred and twenty to one hundred and thirty. We stripped down to our shorts. Union agreed with Tuttle . . . we'd work a half hour, then rest for a half hour . . . drink pints of water, chew on ice kept in barrels near the blower tubes. Can't work long in that kind of heat. . . ." He paused and took three rattling breaths. "But Tuttle kept his foreman on our backs . . . wouldn't keep to that agreement. Waited till somebody passed out before he'd call for rest. And usually no ice sent down from up top."

"Why didn't you quit and go somewhere else?"

"I was going to . . . but found out by then I was sick . . . couldn't get hired in no other mine." His eyes seemed to be focusing better as the food began to have a restorative effect, offsetting Madam Turney's Elixir.

Sturm ate another spoonful and washed it down with a swallow of beer. "Funny thing is . . . the harder the foreman pushed us, the less good ore we took outta there."

"How could you tell until it was milled and smelted?"

Sturm looked at him with disdain. "Mister, I been a miner for a lot of years. I know rich ore on sight . . . by color, by feel. What we took out of there . . . the past few months was poor-grade stuff. Have to move a lot of rock and clay to get any good metal outta that."

"I reckon Tuttle was desperate, then, to keep cutting back on overhead expenses to see if he could strike something better." It seemed entirely logical to Ross that a hard, ruthless mine owner would act that way. Yet he could understand Sturm's complaints as well. The man had taken a chance, been well paid to do a dangerous job, and had ruined his health as a result.

Sturm finished his food and drained the beer.

"Can I help you home?" Ross offered. This man was in no shape to be picketing on the street. The next person might take offense at his sign. "Where do you live?"

"Back room of a house down the block."

Ross helped him up, pocketing the bottle of elixir, and handing the miner his sign.

Sturm leaned on him as they left the saloon and walked the block to the frame building. He helped him inside the unlocked door. The sick man sagged down on his bunk, muttering his thanks for the help and the food. He seemed to fall into a doze almost immediately.

Ross gazed down on him for a moment to be sure he was breathing normally, spread a blanket over the fully dressed man, then turned to leave.

He was startled by a movement on the other side of the room. A stocky man dressed in long johns rolled out of a bunk next to the far wall.

"Oh, sorry," Ross said. "Didn't know anyone else was here."

"John Rucker, his roommate. Thanks for bringing him home." He reached for shirt and pants hanging on the bedpost.

"Gil Ross. I saw him on the street and he looked to be in pretty rough shape."

"Rough is the word, all right," Rucker said, shrugging muscular shoulders into his galluses. "I agreed to stay with Jake and look after him for whatever time he has left . . . which ain't long, I'm guessing."

"What's wrong with him? I bought him some food and he was telling me a tale. . . ."

"He let you buy him lunch? I'm surprised. He has money . . . a small union pension . . . and a lot of pride." He sat down on the bunk to pull on his heavy socks and brogans. "Jacob has what the doctor calls silicosis. Lungs are ruined from breathing rock dust. He ain't the first to get it, and sure as hell won't be the last."

"He was blaming Avery Tuttle for it."

Rucker looked up sharply, finished tying his shoes, then rose and came across the room.

"What did he tell you?"

Ross repeated Sturm's story.

"Hmmm. . . ." Rucker smoothed his sweeping mustache as he stared out the window

at the dreary, man-made hills of spoil a quarter mile behind the house.

"Ross . . . Ross . . . ? Are you that mine inspector I read about yesterday in the *Enterprise*?"

"That's right."

Rucker turned back toward him and seemed undecided about what to say next.

"Basically, what Sturm told you is true. I work at the Blue Hole, too. Fact is, my shift starts at six this evening. I would have kept Jake here, but I was sound asleep when he slipped out. He does that when he gets a chance. I don't want him to get hurt. He's too weak to pick a fight, except by what he says, along with that sign he carries. He's dying and he's bitter. Accuses Tuttle of damned near everything that's wrong with the world."

"Can't say as I blame him, if this Tuttle is really that bad."

Rucker hesitated again. "Did you help Jake because you were trying to get information from him about the mine?"

"Partially. But I also saw a down-and-outer who needed help, and I gave him a hand before somebody came along and kicked him because of that sign he was holding."

"Who you inspecting these mines for?"

"The government. I'm to report on the state of mining in general and give an estimate of mineral prospects on the whole Comstock."

Rucker considered this for a moment. "If I let you in on something, do I have your word that you'll keep quiet about where you got the information?"

"You have my hand on it." He gripped the miner's rough palm.

"This Tuttle is scum, all right, but for reasons besides what Jake told you."

Ross leaned against the upright post of the bunk bed and listened.

"We've talked about Tuttle at our union meetings, and been gathering evidence to set the law on him. Some of our miners suspect he's actually salting that worthless dirt and rock with high-grade silver ore, once the stuff is hauled topside. We haven't actually caught anybody in the act of doing it yet. But Jake came close. Just before he had to quit, he heard a shotgun blast in one of the tunnels, went to investigate, and found the tunnel wall peppered with flecks of gold somebody had shot into it. The gold hadn't been there a half hour before. The stock of the Blue Hole has been rising in San Francisco. When it gets up to where Tuttle wants it, he'll likely sell out."

"If you give me the evidence, I'll expose him and save the union from doing it." If there was anything Ross hated — even more than an upfront, armed robber — it was a sneak thief and a cheat. And this man was a brutal owner besides. He'd be glad to take the risk of exposing him.

"We'll take care of Avery Tuttle," Rucker said. "I thought all this would come to light before now anyway, since *The Territorial Enterprise* has run some stories accusing the editor of *The Gold Hill Clarion,* Frank Fossett, of salting mines. Fossett is a one-third owner of the Blue Hole."

Ross tried not to show his surprise. Using only rumors, Clemens had accidentally accused the right man in print.

"And that's not the end of Tuttle's dirty tricks," Rucker went on, pacing the floor in agitation. "We ain't got proof yet, but we're pretty sure Frank Fossett, Avery Tuttle, and Ben Holladay, owner of the Overland Stage Line, are all in on a plot to force Wells, Fargo to sell out their Pioneer Line that runs between here and San Francisco. Holladay has a reputation as a ruthless businessman. It won't be the first competitor he's forced to knuckle under. Once he gets the Pioneer Line, he'll have a complete monopoly of staging from Kansas to Montana,

Denver, Salt Lake, and clear to the West Coast."

"Why would he want that fairly short Wells, Fargo line?"

Rucker shrugged. "Men like Holladay got all the damned money they could ever spend. But rich men never get out of the habit of wanting more. Since the Comstock's been booming, that Pioneer Line makes a bundle of cash for Wells, Fargo."

Ross's head was whirling. When he'd helped Jacob Sturm into the saloon for a meal, hoping to satisfy his curiosity about the man's sign, he never thought it would lead to inside information about a high-level plot involving a newspaper editor, a mine owner, and the proprietor of the largest staging company in the country. He tried to let on he was used to hearing things like this every day. "How were they planning to force Wells, Fargo to sell?"

"Rumor has it they'll just rob the express coaches till the company goes bust. Wells, Fargo guarantees the full amount of any valuables they transport."

"I see. If all this is known by the miners' union, why don't you turn them over to the law?"

"Lack of solid proof, mostly. Been a lot of discussion at the union hall about what we can do. We don't give a damn about Holla-day, but the union'll do everything it can to come down on crooked, brutal mine own-ers."

This was beyond anything Ross needed to be involved in. He was here only to inspect and report. But Tuttle's false, optimistic report on the Blue Hole to inflate the stock and sale price of the mine would make Ross's own report look stupid and errone-ous.

"These stage runs can't be protected well enough to save most of the shipments?" Ross asked, thinking of his own experience a few nights before when he'd helped the driver and guard ward off an attack.

"Reckon not, from what I hear. Too many places in the mountains where a stage or wagon can be ambushed. Wells, Fargo'd have to hire a private army to protect them. Hardly worth the cost."

Ross's mind was already beginning to work on solving this dilemma. It was really none of his business, but. . . . He thought of Sam Clemens and his potential duel with editor Fossett, and the violence against Martin Scrivener. If he could only somehow get Fossett arrested. In a complex scheme like Rucker had just described, and with a number of hired outlaws involved, there had to be a few weak links. Ross determined, for the sake of Scrivener and Clemens, to find and exploit one of those links. At worst, he hoped to throw some gravel into the gears of this well-greased plot.

"I might just be able to help out the miners' union," Ross said, turning toward the door. "Don't worry. No one will ever know how I knew all this. Even without proof, sometimes a man can fight fire with fire."

"I'm obliged to you for helping Jake," Rucker said, following him to the door.

"Maybe he won't die in vain," Ross said, gripping the miner's hand again.

CHAPTER SEVEN

Ross laid down his steel-tipped pen and leaned his elbows on the tiny table in his room at the boarding house. He couldn't concentrate on drafting this report from his notes while everything he'd heard from miners, Sturm and Rucker, was still churning through his mind. Ross was determined to get a look inside the Blue Hole Mine. The Blue Hole was probably not one of the mines he would have inspected on this trip had it not been for his encounter with the dying miner. He wondered if the other mine owners were aware of the activities of Avery Tuttle. If rumors had spread among the miners, he was certain the other owners knew.

Mine owners, like most men of great riches who lived in proximity to the common source of their wealth, formed an elite club and traveled mostly within their own social circle. A few owners and major stockholders lived in San Francisco and other cities. But the majority had vaulted from poverty to unimagined riches. They didn't take their wealth for granted, and lived nearby to oversee day-to-day operations. Tearing precious metals from the earth was a chancy business at best, dependent as much on luck as skill. These men would deal with Tuttle in their own way. The owners might ignore him until he sold his nearly worthless mine. Then he'd no longer be a member of their inner circle. Yet one cheat in the bunch could tarnish the reputation of all by causing a wave of suspicion among outside investors that might be financially damaging. The other owners would have to deal with Tuttle more directly.

Ross sighed and gave up trying to put himself into the minds of these wealthy giants of the Comstock. Somehow he'd have at least to see this man so he'd later know him on sight. But first he had to figure out how to get into the mine. If Sturm had told the truth about the mine being played out, no foreman or owner would invite a mine inspector down the shaft to have a look around.

He stood up and stretched, then put away his pen and ink bottle. Shuffling a sheaf of papers together, he stashed them in a leather grip under the bed. He took his vest from the back of the chair and slid his arms into it, thinking Avery Tuttle had made a basic mistake that could well prove his undoing. He'd mistreated his employees. Dictators throughout history had abused the peasants at their own peril.

A walk to the newspaper office might clear his thinking. He'd nearly forgotten his half-jesting promise to watch Scrivener's back in exchange for the editor's introduction to some of the mines. That was before the torching of the *Enterprise* office. Everything between Scrivener and Fossett was now out in the open. Short of leaving town, Martin Scrivener had no choice but to take his chances. If a rival editor, or anyone else, wanted to kill him, they'd have opportunities.

Buttoning his vest, Ross realized he still didn't have a coat. The spring mountain chill would be in the air again tonight. He'd been on his way to buy one when the sight of Jacob Sturm had sidetracked him. No matter. Plenty of stores were open at all hours. He closed and locked the door to his room, making sure he'd strapped on his Navy Colt, fully loaded and capped. He thought he'd seen some wild camps and boom towns during the California gold rush, but this place beat any he'd ever experienced. From what he could estimate, men outnumbered women here at least seven to one, and the residents ignored all laws of God and man. Not only did they ignore the laws, they seemed to take delight in ferreting out any they'd overlooked and breaking them twice over — fighting, robbing, cheating, killing, boozing, whoring, gambling. Moral principle was no curb to bad behavior; physical stamina was.

The sun was setting over the nearby mountains as he walked along the street. Yellow lamplight spilled out of open doorways and windows. C Street was ablaze for the hours of darkness.

Ross wondered if he should confide in Scrivener and Clemens. They had enough on their minds already. Scrivener could be trusted, but Clemens, on the other hand — well, he wasn't so sure. The reporter was young and impetuous. Yet he'd been a commercial steamboat pilot, which denoted a man of intelligence and responsibility. Most of all, the two newsmen knew Virginia City and the Comstock much better than he did.

Ross stopped. He planned to share what he knew, keeping his source to himself, as he'd promised. Perhaps the three of them should devise a plan of attack to ruin the schemes of Tuttle, Fossett, and Holladay. When the scandal blew wide open and details were picked up by all the big newspapers in the East, Midwest, and San Francisco, *The Territorial Enterprise* would be the most famous paper in the country.

A portion of the brick front of the *Enterprise* building was still blackened with smoke. The tall, narrow window was boarded up. Inside, the pressroom, now cleaned and scrubbed, looked the same as before, or better.

Scrivener's office door was propped open. Inside, Ross found the editor frowning over a handful of copy.

"Did I catch you at a bad time?"

"Hell no! You're a savior. Let's go get a drink to settle my nerves." He came out of his chair and around the desk.

"What's wrong?" Ross asked as they went out the door.

"Been a bad day so far. The usual . . . copy late, and scribbled so I can hardly read it. Damned near everything I've gotten today needed to be rewritten. Pressmen said something's broken on the platen. This is one of those days when I wonder why I ever wanted to become an editor."

Ross glanced at the rutted street of half-dried mud and plowed manure. "You know, for a city that makes noises about having the best of everything, you'd think they'd keep their streets in better shape."

Scrivener looked at the thoroughfare as if for the first time. "We keep it paved with a conglomerate of splintered planks, old boots, clippings of tinware, and playing cards. Especially playing cards. What the drunks don't drop and the dealers don't throw away, the Washoe zephyrs blow out of our two hundred saloons. When the hay gives out in winter, a lot of mules fatten up on playing cards. Works well, all around. Everything in Nature comes full circle and is renewed."

Ross chuckled.

Four doors down, they turned into a saloon and stepped up to the bar. The editor ordered a Steamboat gin. "A holdover from my days as a compositor," he said, sipping the clear liquid.

"A Pilsner," Ross said.

Scrivener put down his glass. "Our old press is getting creaky. Sure would like to try out one of those new steam-powered presses. Joe Goodman is two-thirds owner of the paper. Don't know if he'd want to spring for that kind of money," Scrivener continued, apparently thinking out loud. Ross nodded, as if he could do something about the problems. "Press would have to be freighted over the mountains in pieces by ox teams and big wagons. You know, that old Washington hand press we're using is the same basic design that's been around since printing was invented. About time for something new, I'd say."

"You own one-third of the paper?"

"Right. So I have a good idea of the finances, although we do have a book-keeper." He smiled. "We're raking in piles of money with our advertising and the orders for all kinds of handbills and other printing jobs on the side. Virginia City has already seen several other papers come and go, like the *Washoe Daily Evening Herald, The Occidental, Virginia Evening Bulletin, Daily Democratic Standard* and several others I can't recall at the moment. Even now, the *Daily Old Piute,* the *Nevada Pioneer,* and the *Virginia Daily Union* are publishing but, compared to *The Territorial Enterprise,* they're no more trouble than flies to a lion. We take the lion's share of the advertising, have the largest circulation, and edge out the others for any big news of the region. Even our editorials make the others look illiterate." He swelled his chest with pride. "In spite of a few problems, there are worse things than being editor of such a publication."

"Like grubbing in a hole in the ground for silver," Ross said.

"Amen."

The men stood silently with their drinks and their thoughts while the supper crowd and miners going on night shift surged in and out of the room. The *clinking* of glassware and the rumble of conversations filled the space in the popular saloon. For the edification of patrons, the wall above the backbar was decorated with a life-size painting of a reclining nude. As Ross studied it, he wondered if the artist had worked from a live model. Nothing had been left to the imagination — the flesh tones were soft and alluring, the dark hair framed the face, the full lips pouted, eyes held the viewer with a disconcerting gaze. The woman in the picture was languidly trailing a diaphanous veil across her nether regions, revealing more than she concealed. With a start, Ross realized the image bore a strong resemblance to the woman who'd ridden in the coach with him across the mountains. He could feel himself nearly blushing, as if she were boldly staring down at him. A local

Jezebel? He caught the bartender's eye and jabbed a finger at the painting. "Who's the gal?"

"Ain't she sumpin'? Calls herself Angeline Champeaux. Rumor says she's from New Orleans. Wish she worked here, but they got her hog-tied at the Blind Mule down the street. We can't afford her."

"Oh?"

"They pay her three times the usual wage to deal blackjack and generally keep the customers happy. But where she makes her real money is on the side with select clientele. She's mighty particular, I hear. Not snooty, but just quality stuff and knows it. Priced outta my range, I can tell ya that." The bartender cocked his head back and took a long look — "Mighty fine." — then turned to go back to work.

Ross made a mental note to visit the Blind Mule. He wanted to see if this was the woman who'd shared his coach on that wild ride across the Sierras. Other than curiosity, he had no reason for doing so.

He tore his eyes from the painting, turned to face the room, and leaned his back against the bar. "Something I want to discuss with you," he said.

Scrivener picked up his gin and also turned around, hooking a boot heel on the

103

brass rail behind him.

Before Ross could say a word, Scrivener directed his attention to someone at a nearby table. "Calvin Tibbs," he said under his breath.

"Who?"

"The drunk you spilled coffee on the other day. The one who tried to knife you."

Ross looked. The man sat alone, reading a copy of *The Gold Hill Clarion*. He was shaved and appeared reasonably sober, although a bottle of Old Noble Treble Crown Whiskey rested near at hand. A white bandage showed under the edge of his hat.

Tibbs glanced up and caught Scrivener staring at him.

"They run you out of Barnum's?" the editor asked.

"You busted my head when I wasn't looking, you son-of-a-bitch," Tibbs replied. "A man who'd do that is probably a back-shooter, too." He raised the newspaper and made as if to resume reading.

"What do you find to read that's instructive in that rag?" Scrivener asked, an edge to his voice.

"Oh, I read the *Clarion* to get the news. I use the *Enterprise* to wipe my ass."

"Then keep right on, my learned friend," Scrivener replied, "and in short order your ass will know more than your head ever will."

Ross was in the act of swallowing, and spewed a mouthful of beer onto the floor. Laughing, he wiped his mouth and nose with his shirt sleeve. "Damn, Martin, you been hanging around Sam Clemens too long," he said under his breath, looking to see if Tibbs was reaching for a gun. Men were killed in this town every day for lesser insults than that.

Scrivener was evidently thinking the same. "He's got a Colt under his coat, but he's too shaky to use it," he said.

Tibbs's face reddened, but he appeared not to hear as he kept his eyes on the paper.

"Let's go find a table so we can talk," the editor said. "I've gained nothing by besting a fool in a battle of wits. He was unarmed."

The two men sought a small table in an out-of-the-way corner.

"I don't want to add to your burdens, but, in a way, this concerns you," Ross began. He laid out the story he'd heard that afternoon from the two miners. "Since you and Frank Fossett at the *Clarion* are at each other's throats, I haven't violated any confidences by telling you this. If you and Clemens have already exposed Fossett in print, maybe he's fighting back because he doesn't want it to be known he's part of a larger criminal conspiracy involving a mine owner and Ben Holladay's attempted take-over of the Wells, Fargo Pioneer Stage Line."

Scrivener sipped his gin and looked thoughtful. "What did you have in mind?" he finally asked.

"To begin, I'd like to get a good look into the Blue Hole Mine, to see if it's producing. But I don't know how to go about it. Miners are working around the clock, including a foreman and probably a superintendent much of the time. Don't see how I can slip in. Asking permission would be a waste of time."

"Nobody at the Blue Hole knows you on sight, except that miner you met today," Scrivener said. "If Avery Tuttle is out to unload that mine on some sucker, maybe you could pretend to be that sucker. Then someone would have to let you in to look around to avoid suspicion. No prospective buyer is going to purchase, sight unseen."

"Wouldn't Tuttle stand to make more money if he sold stock in the mine, mostly to investors overseas who wouldn't be likely to come here?" Ross asked.

"Sure. He could be successful doing that very thing, because investors in England and other countries know of the actual concentration of good ore on the Comstock. They'd therefore be more trusting that all mines in this area are rich. Fossett's *Gold Hill Clarion* would trumpet the richness of the mine to help him. But Tuttle would be taking a big risk. If he were caught, he could be convicted of fraud and go to prison. By selling outright, he leaves himself in the clear because he could always say the vein pinched out right after he sold, so it's not his fault. Strictly a buyer beware situation."

Ross shook his head. "If there's a new way to skin your fellow man, some sharp crook is going to think of it."

"The human mind can be just as inventive when put to criminal uses as it can when put to good uses." Scrivener took a sip of gin, apparently not dismayed by the vicissitudes of humans.

Ross silently considered the idea of posing as a buyer. Risky. What if he were recognized and identified as a government mine inspector? At the very least, he'd be cussed at and thrown out. At worst . . . ? He shivered, and quickly dismissed the possibility of some violent reaction on the part of the foreman or superintendent. But Scrivener's suggestion was sound. It was probably the only way he'd be able to see inside the Blue Hole.

"I'll have at it in the morning," Ross said.

CHAPTER EIGHT

"Chester Gibbons, from San Francisco," Ross said, extending his hand to the super-intendent of the Blue Hole Mine. They stood by the hoisting works the next morning at 10:00 a.m.

"Barry Gunderson," the middle-aged man said, eyes peeking between pouches of fat below and hooded lids above.

The night before, Scrivener had said that Gunderson was known on the Comstock as Old Squinch Eye. "He may appear to be putting a hex on you with his evil eye, but don't pay him any mind. In spite of his size and look, the man's as harmless as a garter snake. Just stick to your tale of being a buyer, and you'll do all right."

"I represent a group of Montgomery Street investors," Ross continued. "They've asked me to have a look at the Blue Hole before they make Mister Tuttle an offer on it." He flicked an imaginary piece of lint off the sleeve of his black broadcloth coat. He'd draped his gold watch chain across his mid-section, from one vest pocket to the other. "It's not as if they don't trust the assay reports and production figures," he continued. "But they're astute businessmen and never buy a pig in a poke, so to speak."

"Yes, yes. I understand. I'll be your guide. Come with me, if you're ready."

He didn't offer to provide Ross with a pair of coveralls to protect his clothing. This was evidently going to be a short tour.

"Jorge, stand by."

The Mexican took the bridle of an old blind horse harnessed to a whim.

"We'll be lowered down in the bucket," Gunderson said.

Ross buttoned his coat to protect his watch chain and to conceal the butt of his Colt. He didn't think he'd encounter anyone who'd recognize him. Rucker was the only miner he knew here, but Rucker wasn't on duty, having worked the night shift.

"We both going down in that bucket at the same time?"

Gunderson weighed 250 pounds if he weighed an ounce.

"Yes, the bucket's plenty big."

The iron-bound wooden bucket was battered and scarred.

"That rope's old and frayed."

"Sir, it's safe. It'll carry a ton of ore. I don't reckon we weigh a ton."

"Is there another way down?" Ross asked, playing the part of the timid city business-man. "What if that blind horse runs away and drops us down?"

"That horse is used to this. He never runs. Look . . . he's asleep now. It's easy for him to let us down. Coming back up is when he has a hard time pulling."

"What if the bucket catches on something and tips us out?"

"Well, sometimes the bucket does catch, but nobody's been hurt bad. Had one man fall about fifteen feet and land on the top of his head."

"Killed, I guess."

"No. He was only stunned a little. Wasn't hurt much. Had a buzzing in his brain for a few days. But he's back at work down there right now."

"Amazing. But, if it's all the same to you, I think I'll go down by the ladder."

"Suit yourself, sir. But the ladder's sort of broke in spots, and you'll find it a tolerable hard climb down. But I'll go ahead in the bucket and sing out when I come to the bad places."

With that, Gunderson disappeared down

the shaft, the blind horse walking around and around, paying out the rope. The vertical shaft was about four feet square, rough-sided and dark. Ross looked down and watched Gunderson's candle grow dimmer and dimmer. The series of ladders stood on the near side of the shaft, resting on ledges, or hanging together by means of chafed ropes.

Ross began to regret he'd declined Gunderson's invitation, but it was too late now as the big man was already out of sight below.

With a hurried glance at the bright world around him, Ross seized the first ladder and began his descent. Down he crept, rung after rung, ladder after ladder, solid walls of rock pressing the stagnant air closely about him. Now and then he heard voices muttering somewhere below, but couldn't tell if it was Gunderson warning him of a break in the ladder. The narrow shaft swallowed and distorted sounds. After a time, it seemed he must have descended at least a thousand feet. He knew, in reality, it was probably less than two hundred. Down and down he crept. Was the fatigue he felt the result of odorless poison gas working on him? What if he should fall? He had no fear of heights, but the thought made him hesitate, take a deep breath, and get a firmer grip. He'd carried his city businessman pose too far. His forearms began to ache with the effort of holding his weight. Several more minutes of exertion made him breathless and he paused, clinging to the ladder, panting for air. Cold sweat trickled down his face. The breaks in the ladder were becoming more frequent. His questing foot found two rungs missing, then six or seven. When he felt nothing beneath him, he crooked both elbows around the sides of the ladder and slid down until his feet contacted another rung or a solid ledge of rock. This ladder, as an alternate method of exit, was useless, apparently abandoned to rot — another way for the owners to avoid spending any money on safety.

Finally he reached the bottom of the shaft where Gunderson and three other miners awaited him. The men shoveled broken rock from the ore cars into the bucket, working with no wasted motion, and without getting in each other's way despite the small passageway. It was clear they'd performed this task hundreds of times.

"Stand from under!" Gunderson called as he yanked the bell rope, signaling Jorge at the surface to walk the blind horse and begin winding the hoist. "A chunk of ore might fall out, or the bucket might give way." Ross, busy catching his breath and being thankful he was standing on solid ground, attempted to get a good look at the ore to see if it was actually silver ore, or only loose rocks and earth. But Gunderson pushed him back against the wall until it was safe to move.

Holding his candle aloft, Gunderson led the way down toward the face of the drift where the miners were at work on what he called a rich ledge. To Ross's practiced eye, it was only a three-foot thick ledge of rock, angling across the side of the drift. It bore no resemblance to any silver ore he'd seen before. If it was rich in precious metal, it was not apparent. Then Gunderson held his candle closer and Ross noticed the rock was imbedded with tiny specks of what appeared to be glittering gold dust.

"Get you a couple samples o' that ore, Mister Gibbons," Gunderson said.

Ross broke off some small samples of the ore and thrust them into his pockets.

"We're only a hundred and seventy-five feet below the surface," Gunderson said.

They were standing on a platform of loose rafters and planks, built to allow the miners to work the higher side of the tunnel.

"If you like, we'll go down below and take

a look at the lower drift," the big man said. "The men have just struck a rich ledge forty feet below."

"Are the ladders as good as those above?" Ross asked.

"Oh, yes," Gunderson replied seriously, missing the sarcasm. "They're all good, except a couple of them may be busted up a little with the blasting. But there's two miners down there. I guess they got down somehow."

"Actually Mister Gunderson, I believe I've seen quite enough. These samples of ore I've taken will be sufficient."

"Yes, sir. But I'd like you to see the vein where the drift strikes it. It's really beautiful."

There must be rich ore visible, Ross thought, *or the foreman wouldn't be so eager to show it.* He allowed the big man to lift up the planks.

"You men put these planks back in place as soon as we go down," Gunderson instructed the miners. "I don't want any rocks falling on our heads." He fetched a nearby candle and handed it to Ross. "Come along, Mister Gibbons," he said, and proceeded to climb down the unseen ladder.

Ross repeated the name, Gibbons, to himself several times to be sure he could remember who he was supposed to be.

As soon as Ross had gone down a few feet, the planks were dropped into place, effectively cutting them off from the tunnel above, and shutting off all light except the candles they held. And even these were burning low as the supply of oxygen diminished.

He worked his way down the rickety ladders, feeling for every foothold, until the last rung apparently disappeared. He probed about with his foot for a landing place, but couldn't touch bottom or sides. He was suspended in space.

"Come on, Mister Gibbons!" Gunderson yelled from far below. "They're going to blast."

Ross gripped the ladder and probed the empty space with one leg. Hot wax from his tilted candle was dripping down the sleeve of his new coat, so he blew it out and shoved it into his pocket. Gunderson could relight it later. "I'll be glad to come down, Gunderson, if you can tell me what happened to the rest of the ladder. How far do you expect me to drop?"

"Oh, don't let go, sir. Just hang to that rope at the bottom of the ladder and slide down."

Ross found the dangling rope and slid the

last several feet to the bottom. Gunderson re-lighted Ross's candle with his own and the two men walked about ten paces to huddle into a deep niche in the wall.

A few seconds later the blast went off with a dead reverberation. Ross felt the concussion through his feet and air rushed past his face carrying the diabolical smell of brimstone.

Gunderson, in spite of his bulk, was one of the first to reach the shattered ledge where lay a mass of blackened quartz.

"There, Mister Gibbons . . . see it? Did you ever see anything like that? Pure gold."

"I thought you were mining silver."

"Oh, we're taking out both."

Ross held his candle close and saw the glittering specks, as if shaken from a pepper shaker. Once more, he helped himself to a few samples.

Two miners were shoveling the broken rock into an ore car, as the smoke and dust drifted slowly away in the light of their candles. It was no wonder Jacob Sturm had contracted silicosis. No water spray was available to settle the dust; no masks were worn by the men; no fresh air was being forced down the shafts from blowers on the surface.

"That's all I need to see, Gunderson,"

Ross said.

"Then I'll see you up top," the big man said, stepping quickly away and disappearing into a side tunnel.

"Hey, wait!"

The light from Gunderson's candle vanished.

Ross ducked into the tunnel and ran after the superintendent, shielding his candle flame from the breeze he was creating. He rounded a bend, then another. His own candle was the only light. The big man seemed to have vaporized into the hot, dead air. "Gunderson!" he yelled. The sound of his voice was muffled about two feet from his mouth. "Gunderson!" He stopped to listen. His own harsh breathing was the only sound. He hurried on another fifty yards until he reached a larger chamber that branched off into three different tunnels. He gave up, realizing he would be hopelessly lost unless he retraced his steps. Again protecting the candle flame, he turned and jogged back to where the miners had set off the blast. They were gone. Only two half-filled ore cars were there. The wavering candle flame pushed back the smothering blackness only a few feet. He was alone.

As he stood there, realizing his guide had deliberately abandoned him to die, he fought a creeping panic. Calling on his experience, he slowed his breathing. In the close atmosphere, sweat coursed down his face and down his sides under his shirt. He shouted several times, paused to listen, but received no answer. He could feel his heart thumping heavily against his rib cage. He was entombed alive in a silent, airless crypt hundreds of feet inside the mountain. It took all his training and self-control to keep from trembling. The candle flame wavered. Since he had no matches, he had to be careful it didn't go out, so he dripped a tiny pool of wax on a shoulder high ledge and fixed the candle upright to give maximum light.

His knees felt a bit weak and he sat down on the floor, leaning back against the wall until the feeling passed. He wiped his face, realizing he had to get a grip on these emotions. Wild panic would be the surest way to death. Until now, no one had ever deliberately tried to lose him in any underground passages. Slowly he began to relax, but the subsiding excitement left him tired and spent.

If he could keep his head about him, he'd find a way out of here. First of all, he had to accept the fact that Gunderson had probably known all along who he was, and purposely led him down to this depth to abandon him. If his body turned up later, it would be termed an accident — dismissed as some trespasser who'd gotten drunk and stumbled into a shaft in the dark. No, that lie wouldn't work. With no marks on his body, they'd have to say he'd sneaked into the mine, gotten lost, and died of hunger and thirst. He knew unexplained corpses often turned up in mines, so no one would think twice about it — especially if they removed all identification from his pockets.

What was done was done. He now had to put his mind to the task of finding a way out. Gunderson would not block the main shaft because there were miners working in the tunnels. And there were buckets of ore to be hauled to the surface. Other miners — that was it. He had to find a miner who could show him the way out. But this mine had miles of drifts and stopes and vertical shafts. Aside from sheer luck, how could he locate a miner? He listened intently for a few seconds, thinking he heard the sound of picks and shovels at work. But all was silent as a tomb. He could not go wandering off at random, searching. If he found no one, he'd be hopelessly lost. At least if he stayed here, he might be able to backtrack the way he'd come; the shaft he'd descended was somewhere just above.

The thick candle on the ledge threw a fair amount of light, and it wouldn't burn down for several hours. The rope dangled from the bottom of the nearby ladder. He ran his gaze up the rope fifteen feet to where it was tied to the remains of the ladder. Yellow candlelight didn't illuminate anything farther up the shaft to where the plank floor covered him. Could he climb the rope? Apparently it was only a makeshift way of descending. The miners would have another way out; he was certain they didn't climb back up that rope after a twelve-hour shift of breaking rock and shoveling ore. Gunderson and the miners who'd been here to set off the blast had gone out some other way. But Ross had no idea where those exits were, and no way of finding out. It was this rope or nothing. He'd seen men in circuses climb ropes as thick as ship's hawsers. But those men were professional performers in excellent physical condition. And this rope was thinner and more difficult to get a grip on.

He got up and tested the rope with his weight. It was strong enough and well secured to the ladder above. Sitting down, he pulled off his short boots and set them aside. He left the candle where it was to give him what light it could since he had no way of carrying it. Being trapped here was bad enough; being trapped in total blackness would be worse.

Springing up, he grasped the rope as high up as he could reach, wrapped it around his hand, and heaved, pulling up with one arm and reaching above with his other hand. His legs flailed as he attempted to wrap his stocking feet around the rope flicking about beneath. His arm didn't have the strength to lift his body high enough for another grip. He let go, burning his palms as he slid down. This was not going to work.

Shedding his coat, he took out his pocketknife and slit the seam to remove a sleeve. Then he slashed it in two, and wrapped the cloth around each hand, tying it on to form bulky mittens.

Again he tried the rope, and failed. The material binding his hands prevented him from getting a grip. This time he cut off his shirt tail, and used the thinner strips of cotton to protect his palms, leaving his fingers exposed. On the next attempt, he wrapped the loose end of the rope around his ankles to give some upward thrust with his legs. But fifteen feet was a long way, and, before he was halfway, he found himself limp and gasping, arms aching, sweat pouring down his face. He knew he couldn't do it, and slowly slid down to the floor to rest. In two or three minutes his breathing steadied. He did some bending and stretching, toning his muscles for another try. As a young man, he'd been a fairly good athlete in foot races and games that required agility, co-ordination, and speed. He'd never been good at sports that required main strength. Rope climbing required both co-ordination and strength. At age forty-seven, he found it extremely difficult. But, if he were to save himself, he had to do it.

Looking up, he gauged the distance. If he could go at it in a rush without stopping, maybe he could make the top before he gave out. He took a deep breath and relaxed for a moment. Then he sprang upward, yanking the rope hand over hand, wrapping his legs and thrusting upward. He made it up beyond the candlelight and could see the bottom rung of the broken ladder. But he was slowing, his momentum gone. Gasping, his arms cramped with effort. *Oh, please, God!* He closed his eyes and struggled, knowing this might be his last chance. With a supreme effort, he hauled his body weight upward, foot by agonizing foot.

Finally, with a last, desperate lunge, he grabbed the bottom rung with one hand, then both hands, as he swung free of the rope. But victory turned to sudden despair when he realized he had no strength left to muscle himself up onto the ladder. Hanging by both hands, strength nearly gone, he wondered what to do next. The wall of the shaft was within reach of his feet. He swung his legs toward it, bracing his feet against the rough rock. The ladder was stable, secured at the top so it didn't swing. Pausing a second or two to catch his breath, he knew his arms would give out if he didn't take the pressure off them soon. He walked up the wall until his body was parallel to the floor. With his feet braced and steady, he reached the next rung with one hand, then the other. Two more rungs and he was finally high enough to swing his feet over to the ladder. He muttered a prayer of thanks. The first major obstacle was conquered, and he stood on the bottom rung, resting his aching muscles, recovering some of his spent strength for the next step.

Working in dim light, he climbed to the top where the heavy planks blocked the way. They'd been dropped into place and were not fastened, so he crouched on the third rung beneath them, placed his back against one of the two-by-twenty boards, and thrust upward, straightening his legs, the rung cutting into his feet. A single plank gave. He pushed upward, toppling the plank back to one side just as the rung splintered and gave way beneath his feet. The upper half of his body and his elbows saved him from falling, and he managed to lever himself up through the opening.

Rolling over on his back, he lay gasping for several minutes before he recovered enough to sit up and look around. It was then he realized he could see. Some light was reflecting off the walls of the drift some fifty yards away, and he heard the sound of tools striking rock.

He got up, pulled his Colt, that was securely wedged into its holster, and padded toward the sound. Two miners were breaking up large chunks of ore with picks and didn't notice his approach until he yelled at them: "Hold it!"

They both jumped. One man leaned his pick against the pile.

"Both of you are going up top with me. Move!"

"Our shift ain't up yet," one of them said, wiping his hands on his overalls.

"I said you're taking me out of here . . . now!"

"Who are you, mister? Where'd you come from?" one of them asked, sliding his hand down his pick handle.

"Never mind that. Take me to the hoist!"

The man swung his pick at Ross's midsection.

Ross dodged and fired, barely missing the miner, the slug knocking chips from the wall.

The two miners raised their hands, backing away, eyes wide in dust-streaked faces.

Ross's ears were ringing from the blast in the confined space and he couldn't even hear the *click* as he cocked his weapon again.

"Grab those candles, and let's go." He motioned with the blue-black barrel of his Colt, then stepped aside as the men passed him carrying their lights. They led him to the base of the shaft he had descended earlier. The big, iron-bound wooden bucket rested on the floor.

"Signal that I'm coming up."

A miner gripped the bell cord and yanked it twice.

Ross climbed in, keeping them both covered.

A few seconds later, the hoist rope grew taut and the bucket swung up. Ross holstered his gun as the men holding the candles grew smaller beneath him. He breathed a great sigh of relief, although he wasn't yet safely above ground.

About halfway up, the bail of the bucket to which the rope was attached snagged on a protruding piece of broken ladder. Ross was steadying himself with one hand on the overhead rope when he jolted to a stop. The rope began to stretch and grow thinner and harder under his touch as the hoist continued pulling. The bucket tilted and started to tip over.

Before he was dumped out, Ross instinctively leaped for the ladder and scrambled up as fast as he could climb.

The heavy bucket, relieved of his weight, swung free and banged from side to side in the narrow shaft. Ross paused for a second and realized the bucket was now pursuing him, rising up through the blackness faster than he could climb.

His ordeal had left him weak, and he glanced upward at the lighted opening far above. He'd never make it before the bucket caught up. And the shaft was too narrow to allow the bucket to pass without crushing him against the ladder. With sudden inspiration, he grabbed the rope a few yards above the bucket and swung off the ladder, clinging like a monkey. He was carried up and up at a steady pace until he could hear the rope running through the sheave above. To save his hands from being caught, he slid down, dropping into the bucket again shortly before it reached the surface and was let down on a wooden platform.

Wonder of wonders! There was still sunlight in the world above. He sprang out and yanked his Colt. "Where's Gunderson?" His eyes were having trouble adjusting to the sudden light. He could barely make out Jorge staring at him, one hand on the blind horse.

"Where's Gunderson?" Ross yelled again.

"*¿Quién sabe?*" the Mexican replied. "No see him."

From the fearful, dumbfounded look on the man's face, Ross decided the Mexican was telling the truth. The superintendent had likely come out another way, or was still somewhere below.

Ross stumbled away down the hill, hatless, coatless, bootless, squinting in the bright daylight, gratefully sucking in the fresh air. He'd reached the road at the bottom and was striding toward town before he realized he still had his Colt gripped in one hand and that his socks and feet were picking up cactus needles.

He swore with feeling, and sat down on the ground to pluck out the barbed spines. He shoved his gun into its scabbard, and tucked his dangling watch and chain away into a vest pocket. The lumps in his side pockets reminded him he still carried several ore samples.

Like some wild man, his clothes were ripped and dirt-streaked, hair full of dust, sweat plastering the shirt to his back. Miners trudging along the road, and horsemen cantering by, looked at him curiously. They probably considered him one of the many drunks who littered the streets day and night, he thought as he staggered upright on sore feet. But he didn't care how he looked or that his muscles were strained and he was bruised and aching from head to foot. He was above ground and still breathing. Nothing else mattered — at the moment. This battle had now become personal.

Chapter Nine

Frank Fossett eased himself into the over-stuffed chair, taking care not to bump his left arm that was supported by a sling. Even though he carried a small bottle of laudanum in his coat pocket, he took a spoonful of it only when the pain rose to the point of forcing everything else from his consciousness. He thought perhaps he had some nerve damage, although the doctor hadn't mentioned the possibility.

He'd arrived early for this meeting at Avery Tuttle's Carson City mansion. Ben Holladay, owner of the Overland Stage Line, was always a little late so the egotistical blowhard could make a grand entrance. Fossett was feeling out of his depth, and nervous. As junior member of this triumvirate, he took orders without question from the others. Even though Avery Tuttle had allowed him to buy into the Blue Hole Mine at a bargain price in exchange for unlimited space in *The Gold Hill Clarion,* he was beginning to suspect he owned a third of a worthless hole in the ground.

Avery Tuttle, Ben Holladay, and he were meeting at Tuttle's home in broad daylight — not a wise thing to do, in Fossett's opinion. Rumors were already rampant that he and Tuttle and Holladay were joining forces in some kind of business deal. With any luck, no one suspected their deal involved robbery, fraud, and possible murder. Perhaps it was his conscience that caused him to see suspicious eyes everywhere he looked. But those editorials in *The Territorial Enterprise* had accused him of skullduggery like salting mines and of trying to burn down the *Enterprise* office. The wound in his left arm gave even further weight to the latter accusation. By some mischance, a bystander on the street had winged him before he could get away. It was doubtful the man had also recognized him. But Fossett couldn't be sure. He'd avoided going to his own office at the *Clarion* for a couple of days, telling his associate editor he'd had too much to drink and taken a fall from his horse, injuring his left arm. The associate probably thought otherwise, but said nothing.

Fossett knew he'd have to do something

about that damned Martin Scrivener, or McNulty, or whatever his real name was. His face grew warm just thinking about the man. If he allowed the *Enterprise* to continue railing at him in print without denying everything, people would begin to believe Scrivener was uttering truth. He didn't mind being accused of adultery. But salting mines? That was too close to the facts, and might lead to revelation of the bigger scheme afoot. Tuttle's voice interrupted his reverie.

"What'll you have to drink, Frank?"

"*Uh* . . . sherry, if you have it."

"Sherry? I thought you were a whiskey drinker."

"Well, it's a little early in the day." Actually, Fossett thought, he wanted to keep his wits about him while dealing with these two sharks.

Tuttle disappeared into the next room and returned with a wine glass half full of amber liquid and handed it to Fossett.

Tuttle employed a cook, housemaid, and butler, but he gave them all the day off when the three met in his new mansion. He'd complained to Holladay that they should meet somewhere else because it cost him money every time he paid his staff for a day they didn't work. Holladay had dismissed

132

his complaint as cheap carping, and pointed out they had more important and high-priced concerns to occupy their attention.

Fossett sipped the heavy, sweet wine and eyed Tuttle pouring himself a whiskey from a cut-glass decanter on the massive sideboard. The pear-shaped, baby-faced mine owner dressed like a dandy. The fawn-colored breeches, the silk vest and starched white shirt and cravat, the polished boots — his entire manner of dressing and acting seemed to fit with the house and its furnishings. In fact, the man himself was appropriate to the clothes and the décor. Only a scant trace of shaved facial hair was visible on the rosy cheeks and chin, mid-section going to pudge, but belted firmly into place. With thinning blond hair and blue eyes, he looked more like a middle-aged cherub than the devious, ruthless man Fossett knew him to be. Fossett smiled to himself behind the wine glass. With a pair of floppy cuffs, silken knee breeches, white stockings, and buckle shoes, the man would have fit perfectly into the court of Louis XVI, eighty years ago.

No one knew much about Tuttle's private life. He'd shown up on the Comstock early in 1861 with no wife, but apparently enough money to invest in mining properties. Either with money he'd brought, or money acquired, he'd built this elegant mansion, furnished it, and hired servants. The liquors and wines he kept in the house seemed more for entertaining guests than for his own consumption. He made a show of drinking, but a single shot glass of bourbon would last him for hours, and Fossett knew no one who'd ever seen the man the least bit tipsy. Nor did he smoke, or gamble — except in business. What about sex? Again, no one knew. Fossett leaned forward, dropping his eyes when Tuttle looked up and caught him staring. A time or two Fossett had subtly tried to pry into the man's past, but the mine owner had made some joking comment and diverted the conversation to another topic. Fossett didn't trust a man who had no faults. In spite of his sunny, sociable manner, Tuttle gave the impression he was not presenting the real man — he was always on stage. The man had a dark side; Fossett was sure of it.

Tuttle pulled a massive gold watch from his fancy vest and popped open the case with one hand. "Where the hell is Holladay? Always late. He evidently thinks I have nothing better to do than wait around all day for him to show up." He didn't mention wasting Fossett's valuable time as well.

He snapped the case shut, returned the

watch to his vest pocket, and began pacing up and down, once going to the front window and pulling aside the lace curtain to peer out.

Fossett sipped the sherry to ease the pain in his arm, purposely avoiding dosing himself with laudanum in front of this priggish man. The silence was broken by hoof beats *thudding* on the packed street.

"About time," Tuttle said.

Fossett saw the big man step down from an ornate coach and stride briskly up the front walk. A sharp rap. The door was thrust open. Ben Holladay blew into the room like a fresh spring breeze.

"Howdy, gents," he said, removing his hat and flinging it accurately at the hall tree.

"What're you drinking, Ben?" Tuttle asked, the irritated look gone from his face. He always treated one of the richest, most influential men in the country with deference.

"Brandy." The big man rubbed his hands together. "Hello, Frank." He acknowledged Fossett's presence with a curt nod. "A fine May day!" he enthused, accepting the brandy from his host. He sipped his drink with obvious satisfaction and smoothed his heavy, brown beard and mustache. "Let's get down to business," he said. "I have a meeting with my Virginia City agent this afternoon."

Tuttle sank down on the couch while Holladay continued to stand in the middle of the room, an imposing six feet two inches. A ruby ring glowed on the hand that held his glass. His famous tiger-claw watch fob showed white against the dark blue vest.

"First of all, I hear you got yourself shot while torching *The Territorial Enterprise* office," Holladay said, frowning.

"I guess word got out about that," Fossett said, his face growing warm.

"A public fight with some two-bit newspaper editor is not what we want," Holladay continued.

"The editorials. . . ."

"I don't care how it happened!" the big man cut him off sharply. "I know as much about it as I need to know. If you're going to do us some good and share in the profits, you will have to keep your head down. We don't want the whole world to know what we're about. You will continue to praise the assets of the Blue Hole Mine and of the Overland Mail and Stage Company in *The Gold Hill Clarion.*"

Fossett nodded his understanding, noting that Holladay's eyes were set too closely together in his broad face, giving the impression of a very penetrating gaze. Possibly a slight defect from birth that wasn't correctable with spectacles.

The stage line owner turned to Tuttle. "I see the stock of the Blue Hole is rising. That's good. What're you really taking out of there?"

"Very poor-grade ore. My men did hit one good ledge at the sixth level, two hundred and forty feet down. But it pinched out quickly. I slipped into one of the older drifts and salted the walls with a couple shotgun blasts of gold dust."

Holladay nodded, sipping his drink.

"The miners are already wondering how they missed it, the flecks are so obvious."

"Forget the miners. They have no proof of anything."

"I know. But their union is strong, and I've heard talk they suspect me of salting the mine."

"Rumors and speculation . . . the Comstock runs on them," Holladay said. "Nothing to worry about."

"One other little problem . . . ," Tuttle began, seemingly hesitant to go on.

"Yeah?"

"There's a mine inspector in town who works for the government. He was just inspecting a sample of the mines for his report. Never thought he'd want to take a look at the Blue Hole. But he did. The strange thing about it was, he came to my superintendent, posing as a representative for some San Francisco buyers. Why would he do that unless he suspected everything wasn't on the up and up? Anyway, I got wind of his coming and took care of him."

"What do you mean . . . took care of him?" Holladay's voice took on an ominous tone.

"I had Gunderson, my superintendent, accept his story at face value and give him a guided tour. . . ."

"And . . . ?" Holladay prompted when Tuttle hesitated.

"I told Gunderson if this man, whose real name is Gilbert Ross, appeared to notice that no metal-bearing ore was being dug out, or picked up samples of the ore I'd salted, then Gunderson was to lose him in the mine."

"Lose him?" Holladay pressed.

"Gunderson deserted him below the two-hundred-fifty foot level in one of the drifts where he couldn't find his way out, and where the miners weren't likely to stumble on him," Tuttle rushed on, as if in a hurry to finish while he had the courage.

Holladay rubbed his compressed lips and

paced thoughtfully around, his boots *thudding* on the Persian rug. He paused and set his drink on the sideboard.

"Another complication we don't need. But we'll have to deal with it. When did this happen?"

"Yesterday morning."

"Could he still be alive?"

"Very possibly."

"Then send someone down there to find him. If he's alive, bring him out and apologize. Make whatever excuse you want about the foreman accidentally leaving him behind, or whatever. If he's already dead, bring out his body at night and drop him down somebody else's mine shaft. When he's found, it'll be termed an accident and neither his relatives nor his government employer will associate his death with you."

"Good idea," Tuttle said, his rosy cheeks redder than ever. He was apparently as relieved as a schoolboy being let off easy by the headmaster. "I'll see to it as soon as we finish this meeting."

"Now, to other matters," Holladay said briskly. "We must keep the pressure on Wells, Fargo. So far, in spite of losses, they've shown no sign of divesting themselves of their Pioneer Line. I can't make them another offer right now without appearing far too eager and interested. Within five to seven years, the railroads will be extended through here and render most of the stage routes obsolete, except for short, feeder lines. That's why I must make as much as I can before that happens. I'll pick the right time to sell out all my holdings just before they begin to lose value . . . while my coaches are still running full and making money. But," — he paused for emphasis — "I *will* have that Pioneer Stage Line across the Sierras to San Francisco to complete my monopoly. All staging is mine by right. Wells, Fargo just fell into ownership of this line. They should stick to what they do best . . . banking and heavy freighting. If I can't acquire the Pioneer Line by one means, I'll use another. Ben Holladay will be remembered by history as the absolute monarch of the mail and passenger stagecoach lines in this country."

Fossett wondered if all wealthy men had such monumental pride and ambition. He guessed most of them did. Here was a prime example. But he had to ride the man's coattails if he were to gain a good deal of money for himself.

Holladay picked up his glass and drained the rest of the brandy. Then he took two steps and sat down heavily in a padded chair, crossing his legs.

"All right, here's where we are, then," he began, addressing Tuttle. "Fossett will lie low and continue to run ads for Blue Hole stock in his paper, writing pieces that will report on other mining properties in the area, but will always somehow work in a hint that the Blue Hole is really the sleeping giant." He pointed at Fossett. "You'll editorialize, without being obvious about it. You'll say the Blue Hole is the up and coming mine, a prize for the wise investor, or words to that effect. . . ."

"If I get a good offer, should I sell out?" Tuttle interrupted.

"Yes. Then you'll have cash in hand and be rid of the responsibility of running it. When I get my hands on the Pioneer, you'll be free to accept a job as my western supervisor. You can move to San Francisco to escape the hubbub that'll erupt when they discover the mine's worthless."

Tuttle smiled. "I could probably sell this mansion for a good price, too."

"As a silent partner, I own a third of the Blue Hole," Fossett reminded them when the two men seemed to be leaving him out of the conversation.

"Work that out between you," Holladay said. "Just remember, the money you receive for stock, or an outright sale, will come first to me. I'll use it to finance the hiring of more gunmen to go after the shipping of bullion on Wells, Fargo. There'll be so many hold-ups they will have to sell out. Once I get my hands on that Pioneer Line, both of you will be well compensated for your work."

A sharp knock on the back door interrupted them.

Tuttle jumped out of his chair like a taut spring released.

"I thought you said we wouldn't be disturbed," Holladay said, glowering.

"Hold on. I'll get rid of whoever it is." Tuttle hurried down the narrow hallway to the back door.

Fossett heard mumbling voices. A few seconds later came the sound of the door closing and a bolt being shot.

Tuttle reëntered the room, looking more flushed than before. "That was Jorge, a Mex who works the lift at the mine. Gunderson sent him to tell me that Ross, the mine inspector, came up in the bucket pretty roughed up three hours after Gunderson took him underground. Ross was loco, waving a pistol, yelling for Gunderson. Ross took off on foot toward Virginia City. Hasn't been seen since."

Holladay muttered something under his breath. "I can't depend on you to do a damn' thing right!" he exploded. "That'll go into the newspaper or Ross's report. In either case, it'll sink the price of your stock."

"Gunderson sent word Ross can't prove we deliberately did anything to hurt or kill him," Tuttle babbled.

"Did Ross get any ore samples?" Holladay asked.

"Jorge didn't say."

"Any experienced miner could tell if rock or dirt has been salted with gold particles, or if the bluish silver ore has been deliberately mixed with clay . . . physical proof fraud's involved in the Blue Hole."

Fossett saw the mine owner's Adam's apple work up and down in the soft flesh of his neck. "I'll find out from Gunderson," Tuttle said in a strained voice.

Holladay got up and shook his great, shaggy head as if to rid himself of the contamination in the room. "In the meantime, we'll stay on schedule for our next hold-up of the Washoe Express. Wells, Fargo has a coach departing Virginia City for Sacramento and San Francisco next Tuesday noon. I've made arrangements to ship small, easily portable gold ingots in the strongboxes, listed as the property of a passenger. My hired guns will hit the coach before it reaches Strawberry. It's costing more and more to find men with guts and competence who'll take on the shotgun guards protecting the shipments. Costs continue to rise, but costs to Wells, Fargo have risen even higher." He moved to the hall tree and retrieved his hat. "Tuttle, in a few days, I'll be in contact to follow up on this mine inspector business. Good day, gentlemen. When next we meet, I trust all of us will have better news to report."

Tuttle hurried to open the front door for him, and the big man strode outside to his waiting coach.

Through the beveled glass front door, Tuttle watched his guest depart. Finally he stepped back into the room with an audible sigh of relief. "I know men who'd give all they own just to have Ben Holladay cross their thresholds . . . hoping some of his luck would rub off on them. Did you hear him say he's going to hire me as his western division supervisor once he acquires the Pioneer Stage Line?"

"He's a man to be reckoned with, all right," Fossett said, draining the last of his sherry and easing out of the armchair. It wouldn't be long before he'd have to take a spoonful of laudanum. He wondered if his wound was becoming inflamed.

"I mean, the man is worth several fortunes!" Tuttle gushed. "And he came up from nothing . . . one of seven kids of a Kentucky farmer. Made it all on his own. His Overland Mail and Express stretches from Atchison, Kansas to Montana, Denver, Salt Lake, and up into the Oregon country."

"I'm well aware of his fortune," Fossett said, draping his coat over his shoulder and bandaged arm. Tuttle's toadying irked him.

"Besides being sole owner of the country's largest stage line," Tuttle went on, "he owns sixteen steamers on the coast, has a couple of slaughterhouses and grain mills, whiskey distilleries, and who knows what else. I'll bet even he doesn't know what he owns."

"On the contrary, I'd bet he knows *exactly* what he owns. How do you think he got where he is?" Fossett said. "By paying attention to details, that's how. Did you notice how much interest he took in what you'd done with this Gilbert Ross?"

Tuttle was staring into space, evidently still awestruck. "Why do you suppose a man like Holladay wants more? Why's he so intent on acquiring the Pioneer Line?" He followed Fossett down the hallway to the back door.

The editor paused, his hand on the brass

bolt. "Men like Holladay are driven to excel. Ingrained habit from childhood . . . from their first break and their first taste of success. They're slaves to their own ambition, addicted to wealth and power like a chink to opium." He slid back the bolt and opened the door.

"That Ben Holladay is a ruthless son-of-a-bitch!" Tuttle said in an admiring tone. "I could do a lot worse than hitch my wagon to his fortunes."

Fossett turned to him. "Did it ever occur to you to wonder why a man that rich would need the money we could get for worthless mine stock?"

"Ben told me ninety-five percent of his assets are tied up in real property . . . horses, coaches, land, buildings, equipment. He needs untraceable liquid capital to fund this project to bring down Wells, Fargo."

"With all that collateral, he could obtain huge bank loans . . . unless he's already overextended."

"What?"

Tuttle finally began to listen.

"In the newspaper business, I hear lots of rumors. Some of those rumors say Ben Holladay is riding for a financial fall . . . that his whole empire is teetering on the verge of collapse because his reach exceeded his grasp. Buying too much on credit, forcing competitors out of business with cut-rate fares and low prices for his goods."

Tuttle stared at him blankly.

"He has the mail delivery contracts because he used his ready cash to buy off Congressmen. His creditors are also demanding cash, and I hear he's mighty short on specie. I've learned to give only half an ear to rumors. But usually where there's smoke, there's fire."

"Nothing to it. Ben Holladay could buy and sell the whole of Virginia City without batting an eye."

"Have you actually seen his financial records?" Fossett could hardly wait to be rid of the both of these men. But first, he had to take enough of their money to see him through the rest of his life. He was tired of slaving for a living, only to die someday in poverty.

"It's obvious enough to me the man is a multi-millionaire," Tuttle insisted, his cheeks glowing, blue eyes blazing defiance.

" 'All that glitters is not gold,' " Fossett quoted as he stepped outside and closed the door behind him.

CHAPTER TEN

Gil Ross squatted on a sandbar at the edge of the Carson River and scooped water into a wide, shallow miner's pan. He swirled the water around and around, stirring a handful of coarse black material. With each rotation, he deftly flipped some of the water and rock particles over the edge of the pan until only a cupful of water remained. Little by little he sluiced the dirty water and lighter grit out until a residue of fine gold particles had sunk to the bottom.

"Pretty good color," he muttered aloud to himself as the sun shone on the dully glinting streak. "And from a small chunk of ore, at that." He stood up with a groan, stretching his sore back and leg muscles. "Got to get into condition," he said.

Setting the pan on the gravel bar, he knelt beside it to rake out the remaining residue of rock and mud with his fingers. He touched the tip of his forefinger to the wet gold. Some tiny flecks of yellow metal adhered to the ball of his finger. He held it up. "So this is what men kill and rob and cheat and scheme and give up their homes and travel thousands of miles for . . . amazing," he breathed, scraping the remainder of the gold dust into a tiny, black velvet poke. He shoved it into his pants pocket. Then he removed two more fist-sized chunks of ore from the pocket of his new corduroy jacket, having replaced the coat ruined in the mine shaft. Holding them in the sunlight, he took a small magnifying glass from his other pocket and examined the ore.

"Just like I figured," he said aloud. Even without the glass, he could detect the gold particles had been driven into the dark quartz with some force. The pattern was the same — each of the tiny, individual pieces had penetrated to various depths, leaving a detectable path of entry. "Huh!" He slid the glass back into his coat pocket. "Blasted in there as neat as you please, probably with a shotgun."

He'd crushed two hunks of ore to wash out the gold they contained, and he'd retained two intact just as he'd removed them from the mine. If the gold in this rock had occurred naturally, and it'd come from a large ledge that had the same concentration throughout, it would assay at more than $2,000 to the ton. A nice lure for investors. But he was convinced the gold in this rock was no more a natural phenomenon than the gold in his teeth.

He stooped to wash the pan, wetting the toes of his new shoes in the process. His old, worn out boots were still in the Blue Hole Mine, unless some miner had found and thrown them away or was wearing them.

Striding back toward town, he stretched out the sore muscles in his legs and buttocks. It would take a few days for his ordeal in the mine to recede in memory so that it didn't disturb his dreams, as it had last night. It wasn't the first time he'd been disoriented in caves and mines, but no one had ever purposely tried to make sure he could never find the way or means to get out. This reaction to the murder attempt would pass. Meanwhile, what should he do with this evidence that the mine had been salted? Maybe he'd have a talk with John Rucker, to see if any of the miners on the other shift had any thoughts about Gunderson. No doubt the foreman had acted under orders.

Should he give the evidence of this salted ore to Martin Scrivener, or reporter Sam Clemens? Since Rucker had revealed that

Frank Fossett, editor of *The Gold Hill Clarion,* was a third owner of the Blue Hole, this would only add fuel to the feud between his two friends on the *Enterprise* and Fossett. Damned if this wasn't getting complicated.

Besides recording this in his report, he had no idea what to do next. Most of the people in town owned at least some mining stock in some kind of mine. The printed certificates representing these shares were given freely as gifts among friends. As near as Ross could tell, there was no intent to defraud. Almost any stock for mines in the area had potential value. It was only a matter of waiting to see how much value. But what he'd uncovered was fraud on a grand scale that could ruin many investors.

It was a long walk to the river and back, and he was thirsty. He decided to stop at the Blind Mule for a beer, to give himself time to ponder these things. The real reason was to have a look at Angeline Champeaux, the flesh-and-blood version of the girl in the painting above the bar. Was she the woman who'd ridden the stage? Maybe it was just her hairstyle that made her look different.

Although only mid-morning, he found her dealing blackjack at one of the gaming tables. Two other women in the room were serving drinks and food, but his eye immediately caught the brown-haired woman. She shone like a lamp in a dim cellar. One look told Ross this was the woman in the painting, the belle of the Comstock, the independent, high-priced courtesan, who named her own price and her own terms.

Ross went to the bar, ordered a beer, and sipped it as he watched her from a distance. The man at her blackjack table finally gave it up as a bad job, tossed down his cards, and left. Ross sidled over.

"Interested in a little game to pass the time?" she asked, smiling at Ross as she shuffled. Then she stacked and cut the deck on the green baize cover.

"Sure." He straddled the tall stool.

She dealt him a card, face down, and one for herself as well, then flipped each of them a card, face up. He had a four of clubs showing, she a nine of diamonds.

"Hit me."

She placed another card on his stack — the six of hearts. She added the deuce of spades to her own hand. "Dealer showing eleven," she intoned.

Ross peeked at his hidden card — a jack of clubs. He placed two silver dollars on the table. "I'll stand."

She deftly flipped up her hole card — the

queen of hearts. "Twenty-one."

Ross showed his total of twenty and she raked in his silver.

"Again?"

He nodded, cringing, since he'd just lost what amounted to half of a miner's daily wage. But everyone in this town was free and easy with money. Why should he be different? Because he had to live on his salary, that's why. And the government didn't count gambling losses as a travel expense.

She dealt and he bet, trying to outguess her. This time he won and was back even.

Two more games followed and he lost both, putting himself down $5. "Enough for me," he said, pushing back from the table. The mid-morning crowd was light. Since no one was waiting to gamble, he said: "You were the lady on the Washoe Express the other night coming in from Placerville."

She looked at him, and recognition dawned in her eyes. "Yes. Sorry I didn't place you right away, but I don't usually study my customers. How's your leg?"

"Only a few scratches from stray buckshot. Thanks to the whiskey in your flask, it's healing fine."

"I didn't thank you for having the nerve to defend us." She smiled at him and he felt as if he'd been enveloped by a sudden burst of sunshine. "That whiskey drummer was useless."

Ross nodded, slightly embarrassed.

"I'm afraid I wasn't very much company for you," she went on. "But I was exhausted. Been awake for twenty-four hours before I boarded the stage."

"Don't know how you managed to sleep, with all that excitement."

"Once we got clear of them, I was confident the driver and you and the guard would keep us from being stopped."

"Cool nerves," Ross said admiringly. "The way we were being slung around inside the coach, I thought the driver might run us off that narrow road into one of those cañons."

She laughed. "Well, we made it, and I find I can sleep well when I'm moving, especially if there's a storm outside. By the way, my name's Angeline Champeaux." She extended a slim hand.

"I know. I'm Gil Ross," he said, taking the tapered fingers, noting the perfect manicure. A woman with her hands on display had to have them immaculate. He envisioned the rest of her on display, but shoved the thought from his mind.

"Gil, it's nice to see you again. With thousands of people in Virginia City, chances are slim of running into the same man twice." She looked over Ross's shoulder. "Unless it's somebody like Sam Clemens."

Ross caught a whiff of rank cigar smoke and knew before he turned around the *Enterprise* reporter had walked up behind him. "Sam, it must be nice to sleep late every morning and hang around saloons in the middle of the day, not having to work."

"You misjudge me, Gil," Sam replied. "I'm working, gathering news. Just came from watching part of an autopsy, and then attended an inquest. Put me in mind of my own mortality, and brought on a powerful thirst." He had a foaming mug in hand.

Ross chuckled. "So you two are acquainted?"

"Sam and I originally arrived in town about the same time," Angeline replied.

"Angie's too high-toned for me, but she does pass along some news to help fill a column or two."

"At least you don't have to make up those stupid hoaxes any more," she said. "Like that thing you wrote last year about a whole wagon train of immigrants being massacred by Indians." She made a wry face. "And that story about the petrified man."

"Probably not the two best ideas I ever had," Clemens acknowledged. "A lot of people took those seriously. No sense of humor. But when I first started at the *Enterprise,* there wasn't much going on here. Duller than paint. Some days I had to let my imagination run free to fill a column." He chuckled, puffing his cigar. "Not any more. Town's been mighty lively for months. Everyone goes armed, so there's an inquest 'most every day."

"Better take care one of them isn't yours," Ross said, thinking of their previous conversation about a possible duel with Frank Fossett. He decided not to mention anything in front of the woman.

"Now there's more going on than Scrivener has room to print," Clemens continued. "Flush times. Money as common as dust. Everyone considers himself a millionaire. Brass bands, banks, hotels, big quartz mill clean-ups, hurdy-gurdy houses, gambling palaces, political powwows, street fights, murders, riots. Everything is competing for space in the paper . . . stage hold-ups, stock fraud. All the folks who own little hole-in-the-ground mines are trying to bribe me to write a line or two about their likely looking ore, or how their ledges are very similar to those in the Ophir. . . ." He shook his head. "Virginia City has become an amazing place. Prices for town lots are going sky high. As an active, concerned citizen, I considered joining one of the volunteer fire brigades, but don't have time for all that spit and polish and parades. Besides, I'd rather enjoy this rarified air than breathe smoke . . . except for these." He held up his cigar.

"Sam, you rattle on too much," Angeline said. "What you need is a woman to calm you down."

"Is that an offer?"

She rolled her eyes in mock despair. "Sam and I are like brother and sister," she explained to Ross.

"Unfortunately," Clemens said.

A concussion shook the floor and rattled glassware on the backbar.

"That was either an explosion, or one of your frequent earthquakes," Ross said, now rising from his stool and glancing to see how far he was from the door.

"Underground blasting," Angeline said. "Nothing to get concerned about. Happens several times a day."

"That's the sound of money," Clemens said. "When they get through hollowing out these mountains, Washoe will collapse as flat as this floor. But I don't reckon it'll happen this week."

"Is your blackjack table open?" a bearded

man asked.

Ross and Clemens moved aside.

"Have at it," Ross said.

The man sat down on the stool and pulled out a rawhide poke.

"I'll see you gentlemen later," Angeline said, shuffling her deck.

Ross and Clemens nodded to her and moved away. "Tell your boss I'll be down to see him at the paper this afternoon," Ross said. "We live at the same boarding house, but he keeps uncivilized hours, so I never see him there."

"Right."

Ross drained his beer and set his glass on the bar. He started back toward his boarding house to work on his report.

Halfway there, his sore muscles were complaining so much he felt like a rusty machine when he moved. He stopped at a Chinese bathhouse and soaked his bruised body for a half hour in a wooden tub full of steaming water.

Feeling limber, clean, and relaxed, he pulled on the tough tan canvas pants and white cotton shirt he'd bought after his sojourn in the mine the day before. This town was not like San Francisco — no one dressed up. Miners, barmen, merchants, and everyone else seemed to dress for the weather and for comfort. Except for the very rich, clothes didn't denote the social status of the citizens.

Back in his room, Ross sat down to work on his report. He listed all the mines he'd inspected, along with the depths of their shafts, the tonnage of the extracted ore for the past six months, how many ounces per ton were extracted and smelted into ingots. He drew a rough map of the area, locating all the mines, large and small; he would add a more professional map later. Then he launched into a description of the mountains, with Mount Davidson as its principle peak.

This mountain is composed mainly of what miners called "country rock", their name for the common syenite that forms the mass of the mountain. On the east side of the mountain, the common rock is propylite, of volcanic origin. Between these two common types of rock lies a series of fissures containing the Comstock deposits. In general, this series of fissures is about four miles long and from one hundred to fifteen hundred feet in width. These rents were caused by an uplifting of the earth's crust, which had then shattered, the up-lifted crust falling back while steam and hot clay continued to be forced up into the rents, carrying up the precious metals.

Fragments from the edges of the ragged chasm on the east side fell back into the opening and, sliding down the smooth slope of the sye- nite, blocked the fissure from closing. Some of these fragments are massive — one thousand feet long and four hundred feet in thickness. These still rest in the vein, the ore, quartz, etc. having formed about them. The layers are stratified, and the ledges are broken and irregular, underlying each other. In places are found detached patches and masses of gypsum and carbonate of lime. The ore contains native gold, silver, some rich galena and antimony, and a few rare forms of silver in small quantities. Also mingled with the mass of ore are iron pyrites, copper pyrites, zinc blend, and a few other minerals. The chasm in which is formed the Comstock lode was doubtless at one time a seething cauldron. As the digging continues and greater depths are attained in the mines, not only are great quantities of hot water found, but the rock itself is in many places sufficiently hot as to be painful to the naked hand. The east wall of propylite of the vein is very jagged and uneven, while the less disturbed west or *syenite wall of the rest is quite regular, descending to the eastward at an angle of thirty-five to fifty degrees, being throughout quite smooth and covered with a heavy coating of clay.*

Hot springs abound through the region and the geology continues to evolve. For the foreseeable future, the amount of gold and silver being taken from the Comstock will, taken as a whole, continue to increase. Based on my experience and judgment, the greatest deposits of precious metals remain to be found.

Ross put down his pen, got up, stretched, and walked around the room, stopping to stare out the window. How much of what he was writing was based on fact, and how much on speculation? He would stake his reputation and his life on the prediction that this area would be vastly productive for at least another fifty years.

He sat back down at the table and dipped his pen into the ink bottle. He continued to write, revise, and edit until mid-afternoon.

Finally satisfied for the time being, he put his writing materials under the bed and slipped on his corduroy jacket.

He'd had several hours to ponder his alternatives. His course of action was finally decided by the mental image of the dying miner, Jacob Sturm. He strode down the street two blocks to the rented room where Jacob Sturm lived. Ross was in luck. The roommate, John Rucker, was there, and awake.

"Come in," the miner said, answering the knock and holding the door open.

"How is he?" Ross asked, nodding at the sleeping Sturm in his bunk.

Rucker shook his head, and guided Ross to the other end of the room before he spoke. "I'm doing all I can, but I doubt he'll last out the week. The doc gave me some pain medicine to ease him along."

"Is he still drinking that damned elixir?"

Rucker nodded. "If he wants it, I let him have some. Can't hurt anything now. He says it helps."

"Can I get anything for him . . . or for you?"

"No. When he wakes up, I'll give him some food before I go to work."

"You're really the one I came to see," Ross said. "Wanted to ask if any of the miners said anything about Gunderson trying to lose me in the Blue Hole." Ross briefly related his experience in the mine, and his eventual escape.

"I heard someone pulled a gun on two of

the men and forced them to take him to the main shaft hoist. So that was you?"

"Yeah."

"Jorge said you came up, yelling for Gunderson. I don't blame you. Gunderson showed up later . . . from another exit, like a damned prairie dog. Told the two miners you'd somehow wandered off and got separated and he wanted to apologize. Said he was going to look for you to see what you thought of the mine as a prospect for your buyers. I think he called you by another name."

"Gibbons. I made out to represent some buyers from San Francisco," Ross said. "So that's the way he's going to play it . . . deny everything and make out like it was all an accident. And I can't prove otherwise." Ross reached into his coat pocket. "But I have something else here that will put pressure on the management and owners of the Blue Hole."

He showed Rucker the ore samples he'd picked up, and explained he'd concluded the mine had been salted.

Rucker took the magnifying glass and the lumps of ore to the window and examined them in clear daylight. "No doubt about it," Rucker said, handing back the rock. "Might fool a layman who's looking to buy a gold mine, though."

"When's the next union meeting?"

"Tomorrow night. Want me to tell them you've got some hard evidence?"

"Sure. And tell them to keep their eyes open for this while they're digging."

"We're searched when we come off our shifts, to be certain we don't steal any rich ore."

"That's all right. I have some right here. If the editor of the *Enterprise* agrees, everything I told you will appear in the next edition of the paper. That should force some kind of reaction."

"Why don't you give me that ore and let me show it at Union Hall?"

"Mining is your livelihood. I'm a mine inspector. Let me and the newspaper editor fight this battle. If we win, everybody will benefit, and no miners will be blackballed."

"You're taking one helluva chance," Rucker said. "Men are gunned down or disappear every day in this town for a lot less than exposing crime in high places. Take my word for it, they'll smash you like a bug."

"They blindsided me once, but next time I'll be ready." Ross smiled grimly, placing a hand on his Navy Colt. "Tuttle, Fossett, and company will think they've stepped into a den of Mojave rattlers."

CHAPTER ELEVEN

Just before sundown, Ross returned to *The Territorial Enterprise* office. Workmen were putting the finishing touches on the restored window and frame. The smoke-blackened brick on the front of the building had been scrubbed clean, the wooden frame replaced, and the tall, narrow pane of glass installed. All that remained was for the frame to be painted, and the place would look as if it had never been damaged.

Ross found Scrivener at his desk and in a better state of mind than when he'd last seen him.

"Where've you been the last couple of days?" the editor greeted him.

"Gathering news for your paper," Ross replied, pulling up a chair. He proceeded to relate his experience in the Blue Hole Mine and what he'd discovered from the ore samples brought out.

"Confirms our editorials were right all

165

along," Scrivener said. "If that superintendent was ordered to maroon you in the mine to die, then probably the owner found out who you really are. Not too surprising when you figure we ran a notice about your arrival and your purpose here. I'm sure a number of people in town have put your name and face together by now."

Ross dug out the ore samples and Scrivener turned up the wick of his desk lamp, adjusted the spectacles on his sharp nose, and examined the rock carefully while Ross pointed out what to look for.

"Yes, I've seen examples of salted ore before," Scrivener said, as if he didn't really need any help. "These would fool most folks, though," he added, swiveling his chair around to work the combination of the heavy floor safe behind him. "If you have no objections, I'll stash these here for safekeeping, just in case. We have your word these came from the Blue Hole, but no hard proof. Though newspapers are not a court of law, we are the court of public opinion. It really doesn't matter if what we know to be true cannot be proven to a certainty." He locked the door, spun the combination, and swiveled back around to his desk. "I'll write up a piece for the next edition." He looked sharply at Ross, and added: "*If* that's what you want. If you'd rather stay out of it, I'll just do an editorial, stating I have proof of the owner's duplicity and fraud. I won't have to mention what it is or how I got it."

"No, go ahead and tell how I got it and that I'm certain an attempt was made on my life . . . an attempt supposed to look like an accident."

"You look a little dragged out," Scrivener said, peering over the tops of his glasses. "Better get some rest. When this hits the paper, Fossett will be on the warpath again. No telling what he'll try this time."

Ross thought it prudent not to mention Clemens had confessed to starting this uproar with a couple of editorials that had hit close to the truth. Scrivener probably already knew Clemens was responsible. And if he didn't, Ross wouldn't be the one to enlighten him.

"It's a shame you have to be pulled into all this," the editor said. "You came to town to do a job and then move on. Now you've wound up being in the middle of a feud, a conspiracy, and a fraud."

"I chose to become involved. After all, it affects my job when the mines are concerned. I know the richer mines are producing well, and the whole Washoe district is one of the world's richest mineral areas.

Nevada will soon become a state in order for the Union to get its hands on the tons of silver it provides. But I have to report it as I find it, the bad with the good."

"All mining camps and boom towns are rough," Scrivener said. "Hell, I wouldn't have it any other way. I could be working for a paper back East and be dying of boredom." He leaned back in his chair and propped a booted foot on the corner of the desk, pulling his pistol, and placing it atop a stack of yesterday's edition. "Keep your Colt handy if you plan to deal yourself into this." He dropped his foot to the floor, took up a pen, and flipped open the pewter inkstand on his desk. "All right, tell me again about your episode in the Blue Hole and where you found that ore, so I can take some notes."

Ross slept well that night, mostly from sheer fatigue. The next morning he had breakfast of a boiled egg, toast, and coffee before taking off at a brisk walk toward Gold Hill. He'd dealt himself into the feud, and he meant to meet this Frank Fossett so he'd know him on sight, then evaluate his potential for danger.

He found the newspaper office in a row of unpretentious wooden buildings. At the front desk sat a young man in a white shirt, reading handwritten advertisements. "Can I help you?"

"Mister Fossett, please."

"May I tell him who's asking?"

"I'll introduce myself."

The man nodded, got up, and headed back through the long room toward the pressroom. Several men were working with composing sticks at a type case along one wall.

A minute later a sandy-haired man of medium height strode toward the front desk. He carried his left arm in a sling.

"Yes?" the man asked.

"You're the editor, Frank Fossett?"

"That's right. Who're you?"

"Can we step outside to talk? It's private."

"Lead on," Fossett said.

Normal precaution not to let a stranger behind you, Ross thought. He noted the editor was wearing a cross-draw holster containing a long pistol. The two men stepped out into the morning sunshine and moved a few feet to one side of the door. No pedestrians were passing at the moment.

"My name is Gilbert Ross, and I'm a government mine inspector," Ross said with no preliminaries. "You're editor of this paper and part owner of the Blue Hole

Mine." It was a confirming statement.

"I'm editor of the *Clarion,*" he replied. "As to what I own, that's my own private business."

"Not so private that word doesn't get around," Ross said. "And your business would be none of mine except for one thing. An attempt was made to kill me the other day when I was guided down into the mine to inspect it."

"All right, I have a small interest in the Blue Hole as a silent partner, but I know nothing about the running of that mine or what goes on there. And what do you mean by an attempt to kill you?"

"I'm sure you already know, but I'll tell you." Ross briefly related the story.

"That makes no sense." Fossett shrugged. "But you seem to be none the worse for the experience. I'm sure it was just your imagination."

"I wish that's all there was to it. As a silent partner, you see the reports of the amount of silver and gold being taken out of that mine?"

"Oh, now and then. Usually a quarterly report. They're doing quite well, actually. Glad I had a little money to invest."

"You're a liar. That mine hasn't taken out enough silver or gold to pay expenses in months."

"Not that it's any of your affair, but they would have to shut down operations if that were the case."

"The owners are pushing worthless stock. Your paper runs editorials about the great value of the mine."

Fossett shrugged, his fair face beginning to redden.

"You're being paid to print lies."

"*The Territorial Enterprise* engages in character assassination as part of their lying agenda," Fossett retorted. "So what? Why do you care? Go report to the government whatever you want to report, and leave me alone, or I'll make you wish you had." His hand slid across his belly toward the cross-draw holster partially covered by the crooked arm in the sling.

Ross saw the movement out of the corner of his eye. "Keep your hand away from that gun."

Fossett's right hand fell to his side.

"I came here to tell you the *Enterprise* will report this week I was nearly killed in the mine, and I brought out some ore samples proving the mine was salted with flecks of gold. If you're not aware of this, then you should be. If you are aware of it, you'd better get out now. And don't be coming after

Martin Scrivener, unless you want me to shoot you again."

"*You* shot me?" he blurted out before he could stop himself. "I mean . . . you would shoot me?"

"How'd you hurt your arm?" Ross asked.

"Fell off m' horse and dislocated my shoulder."

"I think under that bandage I'd find a bullet wound," Ross challenged, not taking his gaze from Fossett.

"Lay a hand on me, you son-of-a-bitch, and I'll kill you, if it's the last thing I ever do," Fossett said through gritted teeth. His face was flushed as he backed away, flexing his right hand.

Ross dropped his fingers to rest on the butt of his Colt. He started to say that he knew of the plot involving Tuttle and Ben Holladay, but refrained. Forewarned would be forearmed. This was enough warning for now. And he'd also thought better of mentioning Sam Clemens. If he could threaten this editor enough to get him to back off from any further conflict with Scrivener, then he'd inform Clemens, to forestall the young reporter's desperate move of challenging Fossett to a duel. Ross had never thought of himself as particularly diplomatic, but the right word in the right place sometimes averted disaster.

"Just keep a cool head, Mister Fossett," Ross said in a soothing tone. "We could have it out right here and now, but what would that prove? One or both of us would be wounded or killed and nothing else would change. I'll be gone from here in a week or two at most. Then you can go back to doing whatever you were doing. But as long as I'm here, you'd better keep your head down."

"Who in hell are you to threaten me?" The cords in Fossett's neck were standing out. "You some kind of undercover lawman for the government?"

"No. Like I told you, I'm a mine inspector. But I don't like anyone trying to kill me, or my friends, while we're trying to do our jobs. So take that as a threat or a warning or whatever you want. But if you try to harm Martin Scrivener, or anyone at the *Enterprise,* you'll wind up filling one of those graves in the bone yard out yonder. Understand?"

The editor looked hate at him, but made no move, nor did he answer.

Ross pushed his advantage. "Remember . . . if anything happens to Martin Scrivener, or his paper, I'll come looking for you. And it won't be at night with a torch." He backed away, hand still on the butt of his gun. Only when he was nearly a block away, did he turn his back and start his walk to Virginia City. The last view he had of Fossett, the editor was standing in the same place, staring in his direction. Ross didn't know if he'd cowed the man, or if he'd only made things worse by aggravating the newsman's hatred. But Ross was all for bringing this conflict out into the open. He was not much for skulking or subterfuge. He liked to know his enemies and confront them face to face.

For a couple of days, that's where things rested. With daily soaks in a hot tub of water at the Chinese bathhouse, Ross recovered from his soreness, wrote a few more pages on his report, and settled into the routine of Virginia City. But he did not relax his vigilance. He never let down his guard, not knowing if Fossett, or one of his men, was going to ambush him. In Virginia City, where gunfire and murder were daily occurrences, it would probably not even make the front pages of the newspapers if his body were found in the street or an alley some night. They'd hold an inquest, a coroner's jury would rule his demise was brought about by bullets fired by "a person, or persons, unknown." Martin Scrivener would probably claim his body and have him buried in the local cemetery. Then the editor would send a letter to his bosses in San Francisco or Washington. Except for his son and daughter, who might come to claim his remains for reburial, Gilbert Ross, within a few months, would be as forgotten by mankind as if he'd never existed. But, as he morosely pondered this over a beer one day in the Blind Mule, he reflected that his belief in an almighty, benevolent God was the only thing saving him from utter despair. Total anonymity . . . dust to dust . . . forever gone and forgotten. It was the fate of every human who'd ever lived, discounting those who'd done something to be written about in the history books. At least God knew and God would remember. An afterlife was his only hope, the only thing that kept him from throwing caution to the wind and going up against Fossett and his kind in a blind rage, and inviting a quick death.

The unsigned article about Ross's near miss in the Blue Hole Mine, along with his finding of the doctored ore had appeared in *The Territorial Enterprise.* In addition, Scrivener had written a scorching editorial about mine fraud in general and the way armed outlaws and white-collar thieves were allowed to do as they pleased in the town, preying on law-abiding citizens. For two days following these newspaper articles, there was no response. And Ross never let on to anyone that he'd paid a visit to Frank Fossett. Ross had taken to meeting Martin Scrivener at the paper and going to supper with him about 9:00 p.m. each evening — a time that was about midway through the editor's working day. They were seated in Barnum's Restaurant one night, having their usual late supper, when Clemens came in and approached their table.

"Martin, I have some news." He didn't apologize for the interruption as he glanced at Ross. "You might as well hear this, too."

Scrivener pushed back an empty chair. "Have a seat and tell us."

"The Washoe Express is leaving tomorrow noon for San Francisco with an extra heavy load of gold ingots bound for the mint."

Scrivener chuckled. "That's hardly news. Nearly every stage out of here is loaded with bullion of some kind. It's public knowledge."

"This one is going to be held up in the mountains."

"Outlaws hit damned near every stage that travels west of Washoe. Get to the point."

"This is part of a plot to force Wells, Fargo

to sell the Pioneer Line."

"Who's plotting?"

"Avery Tuttle, Frank Fossett, and Ben Holladay."

"Speculation?" Scrivener arched his eyebrows.

The young reporter flushed. "No. But I can't reveal my source."

"If you want me to believe it, you'd better tell me."

"Then it goes no further than the three of us."

Both men nodded their agreement. "You got my word," Ross said.

"OK." Clemens glanced around as if to make sure no one else was within earshot. "Angeline Champeaux told me. She'd just finished a tryst with Avery Tuttle. She said Tuttle's not usually a heavy drinker, but tonight he was celebrating the sale of a large block of Blue Hole Mine stock to some British investors, and had more champagne than he needed. She said he drank so much he couldn't perform, so he made up for it by gabbing for an hour, and ended up paying her usual fee, anyway."

"I thought Angeline had more class than to mess with Avery Tuttle," Scrivener mused softly.

"Well," Clemens went on, "she got to pry-ing and he bragged about this plot and the fact that he and Fossett were essentially working for the great Ben Holladay. Holladay will get the money from the stock sale to finance his scheme. He hires the outlaws, and ships the ingots under another name. When the stages are robbed, Holladay splits with the outlaws. Then his surrogate shipper claims reimbursement from Wells, Fargo and returns most of it back to Holladay. If Wells, Fargo has to continue paying out for big losses, they'll soon go bust and have to get rid of the staging part of their business. Holladay is waiting to snap it up at a bargain price."

Scrivener sat silently for a few moments. "We can't risk getting Angeline killed by publishing this, 'cause Tuttle would know where the information came from. Besides, we'd also warn the plotters." He stroked his goatee and stared at the ceiling. "Wells, Fargo will have to know. We won't tell them how we came by the information. They've probably already taken the precaution of hiring extra guards or outriders."

"If the hold-ups take place in the mountains, I assume the Virginia City police have no jurisdiction," Ross said.

"They wouldn't be capable of stopping a group of determined road agents anyhow,"

Clemens stated. "Angie told me Tuttle was putting a gunman inside the coach, posing as a passenger, to make sure the coach stopped and the robbery succeeded."

"Then I think there should be someone inside to nullify that gunman," Ross said.

"Yes, the Wells, Fargo office is only two doors from the *Enterprise*," Scrivener said. "I'll go down there and alert the agent tonight."

"I'll go with you," Ross said. "Been meaning to pay my son a visit in Sacramento. Tomorrow's Washoe Express will get me there in good time."

CHAPTER TWELVE

Ten minutes later, the two men were standing outside the Wells, Fargo office. Scrivener rapped loudly on the wooden door. It was a long minute before they heard the bolt being slid back. The agent edged open the door, gun in hand. "Oh, it's you, Martin." He stepped back. "Come in. What can I do for you this time of night?"

"Got some news," Scrivener said as the agent closed and bolted the door behind them.

Ross saw they'd interrupted the agent in the act of transferring gold ingots from his safe into the four iron-strapped green boxes for the trip west. The two-inch by three-inch by one-inch gold ingots, each weighing a pound, were stamped with the current value of $325.

"Go ahead and talk while I work," the agent said.

Scrivener told him about the scheme

Clemens had relayed from Angeline.

"Hell, everybody knows what we're haulin'," Agent Crawford said, wiping sweat from his brow. "It's just a matter of being tough enough to hold onto it. You can assume that every stage in or out of here has treasure aboard."

Ross watched, fascinated, as the agent stacked these small bricks into the boxes, half filling each of the four chests. He finished by piling the boxes the rest of the way to the top with slightly larger silver ingots. Other small packages and personal valuables overflowed a nearby counter. A big canvas bag of mail leaned against the wall.

"Well, we thought we'd just tip you off, anyhow," Scrivener said, turning toward the door. "I reckon you and Wells, Fargo know how to run your business."

Crawford looked up. "Sorry, Martin. Didn't mean to be short with you. I just had a tough day and it ain't gonna be over for an hour or two yet." He straightened up and stretched his back. "I appreciate the information, especially about the man inside the coach. Keep it to yourself, but we got extra outriders assigned to this run. We're taking all the precautions we can."

Ross wondered why the company didn't

load up individual coaches with treasure only, and send these specials across the mountains with guards as the sole occupants. But that might be just an advertisement for what the coaches carried. Perhaps it was better to have regular passengers. Wells, Fargo very likely had thought this problem through and decided on the best method of operation. In any event, Ross thought, it was no business of his.

"I need a round-trip ticket to Placerville on tomorrow's stage," Ross said.

Crawford gave him a curious look, but silently stopped what he was doing and went to his desk. "You know," he said, as if reading Ross's thoughts, "with every coach in and out of here carrying valuables, coin or bullion, it wouldn't be practical to run only treasure coaches and not haul revenue-producing passengers, too."

As Ross shelled out $45 in gold for the ticket, he could see the wisdom of that. He pocketed the ticket and glanced around the room, noting the light from the low-burning lamp reflecting dully off the gold bars. Ben Holladay wanted to get his hands on this lucrative Pioneer Line that Wells, Fargo had owned since the beginning of the rush, five years earlier. The Comstock Lode generated so much business the company now ran eight coaches daily to and from California. As spring and summer came on and mountain travel became easier, this number was likely to increase.

"Thanks, gents," Crawford said, as Ross unbolted the door and the two men stepped outside.

"How about a nightcap?" Scrivener suggested when they were on the street. "On me."

"Sure."

They retreated to Barnum's.

"You know Frank Moody will be the driver on this run," Scrivener said, when they were leaning on the bar.

"Wells, Fargo's top man," Ross agreed.

"Not only is he fearless, and a damned good shot, but he's a natural on the box," Scrivener continued. "He can turn a six-horse coach in the street with the team at full gallop, with every line apparently loose."

"You'd best have another gin." Ross grinned at him. "Maybe then you'll sound more convincing than one of your editorials."

"I'm sober as a temperance preacher," Scrivener affirmed, owl-eyed. "God's truth. If I hadn't seen him do it, I wouldn't believe it myself. He must have some mental communication with his horses. And the man knows every foot of the road between here and Placerville."

Ross nodded, feeling more confident about this run.

Next morning, Ross basked in the warm sunshine as he stood, waiting for the stage to load. He pulled out his watch. Ten minutes until noon. His Navy Colt, freshly loaded and capped, rested in his cross-draw holster under the flap of his corduroy jacket. A spare cylinder, also loaded and capped, was in his right-hand pocket. In addition, he carried a .32 pistol inside the breast pocket of his coat. Manufactured in Brooklyn by the Daniel Moore Company, the new revolver had a five-inch barrel and held seven rimfire cartridges. His small grip contained an extra shirt, razor, toothbrush, and socks, as well as extra cartridges, powder, shot, and caps.

But at the moment, his mind wasn't on fighting or danger or robbery. It was on the fresh, soft May air and the warm sun. It was positively too nice a day for criminal activity. The benevolence of Nature mocked the whole idea.

Ross lounged against a porch post on the boardwalk across from the Wells, Fargo office and watched the flurry of activity. He savored the moment. Even the likely prospect of going up against armed robbers didn't dampen his mellow mood. He pushed back his hat to feel the sun on his face.

Any onlooker wondering if this stage was carrying a lot of valuable bullion would've had their doubts erased by the sight of the cool-headed Frank Moody who was casually keeping an eye on the loading stage. He was the very picture of skill and confidence, wearing a gray, low-crowned hat, white linen duster over a brace of pistols, shiny black boots, flaring mustache, yellow calfskin gloves, and carrying his coiled whip.

Ross studied the crowd, hoping to pick out the plant among the passengers. But he soon gave up the attempt. Many of the people milling in the street had come to see others off. This was going to be a crowded coach. At least ten or eleven passengers, he estimated. That meant one or two would be riding topside with the extra guard. Several hatboxes went into the rear boot, evidently the property of a couple of well-dressed lady passengers. He found himself wishing this would be an all-male soirée; he hated the idea of lead flying if women were in the way.

Four of the green wooden treasure boxes, measuring a foot by two feet, were carried from the Wells, Fargo office and loaded by the shotgun messenger and one of the extra guards. Each box was locked with a brass padlock. The men grunted as they heaved two boxes up and into the front boot under the driver's feet. With great effort, they swung the other boxes into the rear boot. To all the men and women milling around the coach, it was obvious the boxes were filled with gold and silver ingots.

Almost time to get aboard. Ross took a business card of the Pioneer Line from his vest pocket. On the back of it was a list of the stops and the approximate distance in miles between each. From Virginia City, they'd go down the valley to Carson, then to Glenbrook, up the mountain to Lake Bigler, Yank's, and descend the long grade to Strawberry Valley, about sixty-five miles from here. From that stop, it was on to Webster's Riverside station, Sportsman's Hall, and Placerville, where Ross would debark, spend the night, and return — provided he wasn't wounded . . . or dead.

He slid the card back into his pocket and walked across the street to where the coach was rapidly filling. Two portly men in suits were squeezing in beside two women who were apparently traveling together. The Concord coach was never designed to hold that much blubber on one of its bench seats.

Ross had to turn away to keep from laughing aloud at the sight of the two fat men squirming in beside the obviously irritated women whose well-filled skirts already occupied most of the seat.

Ross stood aside and waited for everyone else to board. He was in no hurry to be crammed inside with all that humanity for the rest of the day. Both front- and rear-facing seats were quickly taken, and the free-standing bench in the middle was fully occupied with three men. The coach rocked on its leather thorough braces as everyone struggled to find a comfortable seat. Ross knew, as last to board, he might have to ride on top. In fact, he was hoping for that very thing. Even the roof would be crowded, he realized. Besides the burly shotgun messenger who'd taken his seat on the left side of the box, one extra guard, carrying a Henry rifle, was climbing up to ride on top of the coach, among various small sacks and wrapped parcels lashed to the low hand rail rimming the top.

Inconspicuously lounging near their saddled horses, a half block away, were two armed outriders who would be trailing the coach.

"You going, mister?" the shotgun guard yelled down at him as Agent Crawford slammed the left-side door against the crush of bodies inside.

Ross was jarred out of his reverie. "Yeah."

"Then you'd best get up top."

Ross put a foot on a rear wheel hub and pulled himself up to the roof, sitting behind the second guard.

Finally, when all was ready, Frank Moody strolled to the right side of the coach, pulling on his yellow gloves. He glanced imperiously around, then swung lightly to the high seat, and laced the reins between his fingers. All eyes were on him, but he didn't make a practice of whipping his team to a gallop on C Street just to make a grand exit. On the contrary, he took pride in starting his horses gently so the passengers were hardly aware they'd begun to roll. In Moody's opinion, voiced to a reporter for the *Enterprise,* jackrabbit starts were for fools and beginners, and were hard on both animals and equipment. He preferred to save his team for the pull up mountain grades, or for outrunning road agents. His whip was likewise used sparingly, and usually snapped only near the ears of his leaders, if they began to lag.

Thus, six horses and the heavily loaded coach began to move as one, with no fuss, or shouting, or cracking of whip. Almost before Ross realized it, they were rolling, the buildings sliding by smoothly on either side, trace chains *jingling,* iron-bound wheels grinding over packed earth. Except for not having anything to lean back against, he much preferred to be up here where he had a fine view, plenty of fresh air and sunshine. He stretched out on his stomach, propping up on both elbows. The extra guard, who laconically chewed a wad of tobacco, sat, cross-legged, with the rifle spanning his lap.

They quickly reached Carson City, but stopped only for a bag of mail and a few small parcels the guard was able to tuck in around luggage in the boot.

Two hours later they were in the Sierras, where they stopped to change teams, without the driver leaving his seat, then were off again, winding along a ridge-top road that was dry, level, and hard-packed. Between the trees towering above the road, snow-capped peaks shone in the distance, with a deep blue sky in the background. The air was noticeably cooler, and Ross enjoyed every minute of it.

Every now and then, on a straight stretch of road, he glimpsed one of the outriders trailing the coach one hundred yards behind. As the miles rolled under their wheels, Ross began to wonder if the safety precautions were going to work and prevent the planned robbery. Surely, in daylight, with two armed guards atop the coach and two more on horseback, no outlaws would chance being shot attempting a hold-up. Then he thought of the plant he couldn't identify who rode inside the coach.

Near the crest of a hill, Moody slowed the team to pass three tall freight wagons; their ten-mule teams and drivers were bunched up in a turnout, apparently resting before they began the long descent northeast toward the Comstock. The wagons were piled high with pipes and mining gear. One of the other wagons carried boxes and barrels of flour, beans, whiskey, and ready-made clothing.

Five miles farther, they overtook another train of big freight wagons, the ox teams plodding westward. Moody rested his foot lightly on the brake and walked the lines up between his thumbs and forefingers, just enough to communicate with the leaders. While the bearded teamsters watched stolidly, Moody eased team and coach past them with hardly a foot to spare on the narrow road. Ross enjoyed watching the driver work. He was a master of his craft.

Seven miles beyond, the team trotted into a long, curving upgrade. A twenty-foot-tall bluff of vertical rock bounded the left side of the road. On the right, a thick stand of pines sloped off into a shallow ravine.

Moody subtly brought the tiring horses to a walk. *"Whoa!"* The driver's right foot jammed against the brake lever. The team came to a stop just in time to avoid hitting a slender pine fallen from a rocky crevice across the road, blocking their way.

Two masked men with rifles leaped out from either side of the road.

"Throw up your hands!" came a sharp command.

Caught on a narrow road with no room to turn and nowhere to go, the two guards were helpless under the muzzles of the rifles. Moody swore explosively as he slowly moved his hands to shoulder height, still holding the lines.

"Heave down the box!" a bandit commanded.

Moody wrapped the lines around the brake handle and leaned forward. "Gimme a hand with this," he muttered to the shotgun messenger as he reached below his feet into the boot.

"Hear tell you got four treasure boxes this trip," one of the masked men said, laughing.

The driver and guard gripped a handle on either side of a box and heaved it up and out, letting it fall to the dirt with a *thump.*

"Well, well! That sounds like it's full of something almighty heavy. Gold, maybe?" the talkative robber said.

"Rocks," Moody said.

"We'll see about that," the robber said. "If it's rocks, I'll leave your guts inside this box for your boss to find."

"Quit jawing and get to it!" the shorter of the two bandits growled.

"Shut up! I'm a man who enjoys his work," the first one shot back. Then he motioned with his rifle. "Now the other box. Toss it off on the right side."

Ross heard some commotion at the rear of the coach and looked to see two more bandits on foot throwing back the leather flap of the rear boot. They had to holster their guns to lift out the two heavy treasure boxes. Ross gritted his teeth in frustration. In spite of all the precautions, the hold-up was going off without a hitch so far. He heard no sound from within the coach. The bandit posing as a fare-paying rider was likely holding a gun on the other passengers, nullifying any resistance from them.

A rifle *cracked* from behind them. One of the bandits dropped his end of the load and toppled over onto the box. The other bandit jerked his pistol and fired two shots at the following outriders, sixty yards back, who were in the act of leaping off their mounts and taking cover on each side of the road.

The two masked robbers near the front of the coach dashed back into the heavy stand of trees on the right. The long pine across the road blocked the team and coach from moving, but the horses panicked at the explosions of gunfire, jumping and tossing their heads. Nobody was at the reins as Moody was crouching low in the front boot, long pistol jumping in his hand as he fired at the fleeing bandits in the thick stand of pines.

Ross felt the guard next to him flop down and heard the ratcheting of the Henry's lever. The battle was on. Without being aware of drawing his gun, Ross had his Colt in hand and fired down at the distracted robber behind the coach. But it was a snap shot and the slug *spanged* off the iron rim of the rear wheel. Suddenly aware of danger from both directions, the masked outlaw dived under the tall coach.

The shotgun messenger jumped down from his seat to recover his short double barrel from the ground. Just as he snatched it up and turned, he caught a slug in the knee from the outlaw under the coach. He crumpled to the ground. A hand with a gun thrust out the coach window. A tongue of flame darted from the muzzle and the guard, who was struggling to crawl to cover, flopped over on his back.

Individual shots exploded into a general roar, nearly drowning screams from inside the stage. Slugs ripped rough chunks of bark from thick pines. Bullets struck splinters from the top edge of the stage as the hidden gunmen zeroed in on Ross and the guard atop the coach. Flat on his belly, Ross felt very exposed and dared not move. But they were something of a moving target, Ross realized, feeling the coach jerking. The brake was set, but the rearing and plunging of the squealing team set the coach to rocking and sliding.

Ross heard the muffled *boom* of a shot beneath him. The bandit inside was shooting at someone. Another blast from below and a slug tore through the roof next to his elbow. The inside plant was trying to clean off the top of the coach!

Furious, Ross sprang off the roof, flexing his knees to cushion the landing, rolling to the ground and then to his feet in one fluid motion. He thrust his Colt inside the coach window. A well-dressed fat man was in the act of firing another shot upward through the ceiling. Ross eared back the hammer and shot him pointblank in the side, filling the coach with burned powder smoke as the passengers cringed from the blast.

Suddenly Ross felt something burn his left heel. The man underneath! Ross leaped to his right and rolled behind the legs of the nervous horses. Lying flat, arms extended, he fired once, then was blinded by a hoof scuffing dirt into his eyes. He frantically blinked his watering eyes to clear his vision as the robber fired at him. But the slug was deflected by a spoke in the front wheel. Ross got off another shot. Through blurred vision, what appeared to be a dark blob stopped moving. As his watering eyes began to clear, Ross saw the robber lying still under the coach.

The firing became sporadic, and then stopped. Ross's ears were ringing from the explosions, as he moved away from the *thudding* hoofs. How many more were there? He tried to make a quick count, but his mind was in a whirl. At least two in front and two in back. The ones in front had gotten away into the trees, probably where their horses were tied. The two in back were down. The outriders had gotten one and he'd gotten the other, plus the man inside the coach.

The shotgun guard was lying nearby, probably dead, or close to it. Ross got cautiously to his feet, carefully wiping the remaining dirt from his eyes.

Moody was back on the box. "*Whoa! Easy!*" His mellow voice had a calming effect on the team as he drew on the reins. But the horses were still stamping and walling their eyes.

Ross heard the sound of receding hoof beats in the timber as the two remaining bandits made their getaway.

By some miracle, the guard atop the coach had not been hit and climbed down, being careful not to touch the hot metal of his Henry rifle.

Ross opened the coach door. "Everyone all right?"

A woman was slumped in the seat. "She just fainted," the second woman said, reaching for Ross's hand to climb out. Her knees nearly buckled, and she sat down weakly on the ground, her face drained of color.

The rest of the male passengers got out and Ross went to confer with the guard who was examining the shotgun messenger on the ground. "Dead," he stated, straightening up. "Well, we got three of them, and they got one of us," he summarized with a grim look on his face. "Helluva human price, but these bandits keep right on trying."

"The four boxes are safe," Ross said. "Three on the ground and one still in the rear boot." He swung up his Navy Colt at the sound of hoof beats. But it was only the uninjured outriders reining up close by.

With the team under control, Moody stepped down to join them. He took off his hat and wiped a sleeve across his brow. Drawing a deep breath, he looked from one to another. "Get the bodies up top and lashed down," he said, returning to practicalities. "Reload the treasure boxes." He reached inside his duster and pulled out a flat flask. "Anybody wants, can have a jolt of this forty-rod to brace up. Make sure the passengers are all right, while I check the horses. Then a couple of you help me secure a line to the lower end of that pine across the road, and we'll tie off to the coach. I'll back the team down slowly and we'll drag that tree out of the way far enough to go around."

"I'm not sure Wells, Fargo pays me enough to do this job," the guard said, leaning his Henry against the coach. He reached underneath to drag out the body of the robber.

Moody gave a tight-lipped smile. "You could be humped over a ledger somewhere, ruining your eyesight for half the money."

"You got a point."

Ross felt a wetness on his ear and put his hand to it. His fingers came away bloody. He took his bandanna and carefully pressed it to the earlobe that began to sting where the bullet had clipped it. Blood dripped on the shoulder of his jacket.

As the adrenaline ebbed, he noticed he was limping, unable to put weight on his left foot. Sitting on the ground, he removed his shoe and sock. The flesh on the inside edge of his heel was purpling, but the slug had not penetrated his foot, only grooved the hard leather edge of the shoe's heel. "Lucky," he muttered, putting his sock and shoe back on.

A total of four men were dead, and one of the male passengers had a slight wound in his calf muscle where a bullet had penetrated. The stage was riddled with holes. But the four treasure boxes were intact and Ben Holladay's plan had been dealt a sharp setback.

"Where'd they hit you?" one of the outriders asked, seeing Ross holding a bloody bandanna to his head.

"Just nipped my earlobe and my heel."

The lean, wind-burned rider spat out the used-up lump of chewing tobacco stored in his cheek. "Hell, I been bit worse by bedbugs."

Ross ignored the jibe, pocketed the bandanna, and reached into his coat pocket for his spare cylinder. He saved the empty one, and felt to be sure his .32 back-up pistol hadn't fallen out of his inside breast pocket. It was still a long way to Placerville.

CHAPTER THIRTEEN

Once the coach was again under way, it carried a mostly subdued, shaken group of people. Four bodies lay on the roof, tied side-by-side to the hand rail. Moody had covered them with a well-worn roll of canvas he used to protect parcels in the front boot.

While inspecting his team, Moody had discovered a bullet crease across the rump of one of the wheelers, but the wound was superficial. The guard with the Henry rifle took the place of the dead shotgun messenger on the box beside the driver.

Ross rode inside, seated next to the woman who'd been revived from her swoon. He occupied the seat of the outlaw he'd killed.

As Moody pushed the team along the level road, then down the long, gradual grade, Ross began feeling queasy. Normally the rocking motion of the coach, even when someone was smoking a cigar, didn't bother his stomach. He turned his face toward the breeze blowing in the window and tried to concentrate on imagining himself relaxing by a lake in fresh air and bright sunshine. This had worked in the past to keep him from vomiting. But his thoughts kept returning to the fight as he replayed the gun battle, step by slow step. He began to realize his stomach distress was a reaction to having shot and killed a man — something he'd never done before. Regardless of how justified this was, he couldn't get around the fact that he'd taken a human life. If he could've gotten the drop on the man to arrest him, or maybe only wounded him. . . . Ross leaned closer to the open window for fresh air. He'd been fighting for his life and the lives of others, and had no time to think — only time for reflex action. He didn't even know the man's name. After the fact, he regretted his decision to deal himself into this situation. It was really none of his affair. He took a deep breath and leaned back against the leather seat, feeling drained.

The wounded man was a miner on his way to San Francisco to see relatives. One of the men had helped rip the miner's pants leg up high enough to expose the bullet hole, then tied a bandanna around the wound, which had minimal bleeding. The bullet had penetrated his calf, lodging too deep to be extracted without a sharp knife. The man shouldn't have tried to resist the undercover robber once he had drawn his gun.

No one spoke; everyone was lost in thought. Two of the men kept consulting their watches and looking out the windows at the sun declining behind the mountains, evidently hoping to reach Strawberry Valley soon. Ross managed to fall into an exhausted doze, heedless of any potential danger from another hold-up down the road.

Without further incident, the stage rolled into Strawberry Valley station at dusk. The four bodies and the bullet-riddled stage caused a stir among even the hardened teamsters and miners who'd stopped to lodge at the three-story inn. The station-keeper, John Barry, ordered the dead hauled to a storage room at the rear. He announced the remains would be shipped back to Virginia City on the next eastbound freight wagon, or stage, at Wells, Fargo expense.

After a short supper and a change of teams, the driver, new shotgun guard, two outriders, and most of the passengers, running more than an hour behind schedule, would continue on to Placerville. During supper, the dining room was abuzz with conversation about the attempted robbery.

Both women passengers and one of the men decided they'd had enough for one trip and elected to remain at the Strawberry Valley station overnight. Since the lodge was nearly full, Barry gave the last available room to the women — a cubbyhole under the eaves on the third floor, while Ross and the other male passenger would be relegated to the floor of a storage room off the dining hall.

Still feeling queasy, Ross avoided the noisy company at the dining tables and went into the barroom for a beer to settle his nerves and stomach. Other men filtered into the bar and Ross overheard snatches of conversation about the hold-up. It was mostly garbled facts they'd culled on the fly from those who'd gone on with the stage.

Two red-shirted men leaned on the polished mahogany a few feet away.

"Say, mister, your name Ross?" the younger of the two asked.

Ross cringed inwardly. "That's right."

"Hear tell you blasted hell outta them road agents," the taller man said.

"Who said that?" Ross was startled out of his lethargy.

The taller man yanked a thumb over his

shoulder. "Those two women passengers and that chubby gent with them. Said it hadn't been for you, those robbers would've killed more of you and gotten away with the treasure boxes, too."

Ross twisted to look over his shoulder at the man and the two women. "Well, it wasn't quite like that." He hoped these two would get discouraged and leave. He was in no mood to be sociable.

"We got the blow by blow of what happened, and they say you're a hero," the younger man insisted. "Saved their lives when you shot that fella inside the stage."

"I was just trying to save myself," Ross said.

"I'd be proud to buy you a drink, Mister Ross."

"The name is Gil."

"Barkeep, another of whatever Gil is drinking."

A foaming pint was slid down the bar.

"Gents, I appreciate this, sure enough," Ross said, "but I'm no hero. I was just fighting like the driver and guards. Those five robbers had us cold, from front and back and inside the coach. And the road was blocked with a tree. If anybody deserves credit, it was those two outriders who came up, shooting." Ross didn't know what the passengers had told these men, but he might as well tell the facts of what happened from his own perspective. "Once the outriders opened fire and killed one of the robbers, the others were distracted. The two masked men up front jumped for cover in the trees to avoid rifle fire from the rear. Then the two guards, the driver, and I saw our chance to put up a fight."

"One of those ladies said you stuck your gun in the coach window and shot the man who'd been holding them at gunpoint. Then she fainted and didn't know nothing else until she come to after the fight was over. She said that was the most courageous thing she'd ever seen, what with that robber trying to shoot through the roof and all."

Ross glanced toward the three at a table just inside the door. The younger, more attractive of the two women, smiled at him. He turned back to the bar. Now wasn't the time. "Look, gents, I'll give a report on all this to Wells, Fargo, but right now I'm really tired and I want to go clean up and get this ear tended to."

"Yeah, you got bloodied up some," the taller man said admiringly. "Are you a company guard, too?"

"No. Just a passenger." He started to urge them to split the untouched beer in front of

205

him, but then thought better of it. In this country, some men who bought drinks took it as a deadly insult if a stranger refused their hospitality. And he wanted no more conflict just now. He finished his first beer and started on the second.

"Tell us how it happened, Gil. Give us the details," the younger man urged.

Since he was drinking on them, Ross thought he'd better oblige. He didn't want to go over it again, but he'd been replaying the details in his mind ever since it had happened anyway.

"All right, just this once. Then I have to go." He started at the beginning of the trip and gave them a somewhat abbreviated summary of the attempted hold-up, downplaying his own rôle. "And that's about it, gents." He drained his glass. "No more to tell. Now I've got to go. Thanks for the beer." He slid away from the bar feeling full and gaseous after two pints on an empty stomach. He wondered if he should have gone on to Placerville where he could have easily found a hotel room for the night. But he felt a need to get back to Virginia City as soon as possible.

He found John Barry, who was overseeing the kitchen help, and inquired about some soap and water.

"You need more than that," Barry said, glancing at the dried blood on his head and coat. "Set you down over there, and I'll fetch my wife, Edith. She'll fix you right up."

And Edith did fix him up. She gently washed his head with warm water and, using linen thread and a small needle, took two stitches to close the wound in Ross's earlobe. "You'll be a might shorter on that side now," she said, putting away her sewing kit.

"Nothing about me is symmetrical, anyhow." He smiled.

"You'll want to snip those threads and pull them out in a few days," she added, as if her duties as hostess had included sewing up more wounds than hems or buttons on shirts.

He thanked her profusely. Then he borrowed a blanket. After a trip to the outhouse, he returned to fashion a nest for himself in a corner of the storeroom behind buckets and brooms where he wouldn't be stepped on.

The next morning his upset stomach was gone and his appetite was back, making the soft May morning even more lovely. He was among the first to belly up to the dining table. A half hour later, he came away pleasantly stuffed with flapjacks, maple syrup, and sausages washed down with three cups of coffee.

John Barry, who functioned as a Wells, Fargo agent on an as-needed basis, cashed in the unused portion of his ticket.

The first eastbound stage rolled in on schedule at 8:20 a.m. With only four passengers inside, it was not as heavily loaded and had room on top for the four stiffened corpses. No spare wood was available for coffins, so the bodies were tightly wrapped in canvas and bound to the top of the coach. The driver was a stranger to Ross, but wore the usual Wells, Fargo white linen duster. A small, taciturn man, he looked a bit sour when told he'd be carrying four dead passengers the rest of the way to Virginia City.

The trip back to Virginia City was uneventful, and the stage rolled to a stop in front of the Wells, Fargo agency at 3:30 that afternoon. Ross stepped down, wincing at the pain in his bruised heel.

He headed straight for *The Territorial Enterprise,* two doors away, and found Martin Scrivener just starting his workday.

"You back already? Wasn't expecting you until at least tomorrow night." He glanced sharply at Ross's damaged ear and spots of dried blood on his coat. "Looks as if Angeline's report was right about a hold-up."

"You might say so."

"Tell me about it."

Ross hooked up a chair with his foot and sat down by the editor's desk. "The driver of the stage I just came in on is hauling four bodies and has the tale second-hand. But if you want a first-hand account, get out your pencil."

Ross told Scrivener the entire story. The editor asked a couple of questions to clarify some minor points, then sat for a long, thoughtful moment. "Anybody else come back on that stage with you who was there when it happened?"

"No."

"Then we got an exclusive. The telegraph wire hasn't been stretched to this town yet. This is almost worth getting out an extra edition." He paused, rubbing his goatee. "No, I think not. We don't want these robbers . . . Holladay, Tuttle, and Fossett included . . . to get the idea they're important enough to warrant an extra. Our early morning headline will still be an exclusive. I'll have room if I bump out that two week-old war news."

Ross rose. "Reckon I'll go soak in a hot tub at the bathhouse, and then get some sleep. If you need me, I'll be at our boarding house."

On his way down the street, Ross hardly noticed the normal daily uproar in the saloons he passed. He'd become inured to the loud talk, the hoarse swearing, crashing glass, hurdy-gurdy music, blasts of gunfire, along with the cheerful musical wheeze of the organ-grinder's box, and the monotonous *rumble* of the stamp mills in the distance. Grimly he reflected he now fit in with all these worst dregs of humanity because "he'd killed his man." Often that expression had fallen on his ears since his arrival here, spoken as if it were a badge of honor, a pass into hell's membership club. He was one of them now. The realization made him feel queasy all over again, and somehow dirty, as if he'd committed some unpardonable sin, which forever separated him from decent human society.

With an effort, he thrust the thought aside. What was done was done. The men were dead and couldn't be brought back. Besides, he himself might be the one lying in the undertaker's parlor if that bandit's shots through the coach roof had been accurate — or lucky. So much of life was determined by luck. Some didn't consider it luck or happenstance at all. A few of his acquaintances believed everything that happened was foreordained. To Ross's way of thinking, that denied the existence of free will, in which he was a firm believer. God, in His infinite knowledge, knew the future, Ross reasoned, so He was aware of what any man's choices were going to be. Yet, for Ross, the Almighty compelled no one's actions. If any man wanted to send himself to perdition, he had to work at getting there. He couldn't count on divine help.

Before he realized it, his ruminations and wayward feet had carried him past his favorite Chinese bathhouse.

An hour later, wrinkled and clean, he went on to his boarding house, and began to write up his first-hand account of his experiences on the Washoe Express. Besides the dry report he was composing, he also kept a journal into which he poured all factual details, impressions, descriptions, and characters. By the time he left this place, he could, by selecting, rearranging, and polishing, have a book he felt would sell anywhere in the country. Easterners would be fascinated to read about the Wild West, even though he might have to tone down the reality of Washoe to make it credible to readers who hadn't experienced it in person.

A week rolled past rather quietly. Everyone,

it seemed to Ross, was resting, gathering strength for the next crisis or onslaught, or whatever was to come in the drama in which he'd become a player. *The Territorial Enterprise* had run the story describing Ross's harrowing ordeal in the Blue Hole Mine, and his finding of the ore salted with gold flecks. There was no apparent reaction to the piece. To the average citizen, corruption and fraud were a daily occurrence to be ignored as commonplace. The attempt on Ross's life was likewise nothing to remark about, given the frequency of more direct methods of murder. The article relating the details of the foiled hold-up of the Washoe Express, except for the number of men killed, was also routine. It was considered a dull week if at least five or six hold-ups were not reported.

Lacking identification in their pockets, the three dead robbers were placed in open wooden boxes and stood up in the window of a hardware store with a sign reading:

DO YOU KNOW THESE MEN?

In the two days the corpses faced C Street, no one came forward to identify them. The hardware owner and the local police began to assume the men were strangers in town.

The police chief, Amos McClanahan, thought it very curious not one of the three carried a billfold, or any money, or a receipt of some kind. The fat man had a blue bandanna in his pocket, but that was all. It was almost as if the men were being purposely incognito, in the event they were killed or captured.

In the warm weather, the odor of decomposing bodies began to offend customers of the hardware, so Chief McClanahan paid a photographer to record images of the deceased on wet-plate negatives. Then the city hired an undertaker to bury the three in paupers' graves just outside the fenced city cemetery.

The town council, more in the order of tying up loose ends and showing the outside world Virginia City was, indeed, a civilized place, offered a reward of $10 for each of the dead men who could be identified. This incentive worked. A day after the three were buried, two men who worked as swampers in the Knock-Em-Stiff Saloon hesitantly came forward to inspect the photographs in the police chief's office. They agreed the names of the men were "Red" and Cyrus, and the fat man Ross had shot was a gambler and gunman known to the local outlaw element as "Bilious" Vance. The pair making the identification didn't know two of the given names, but it was good enough to claim the reward, as the police weren't particular and would now have something to carve into the wooden markers.

The shotgun guard who'd been killed in defense of the stage was another story. Jim Sessions was known and loved by many in the town as a brave and honest man, as well as a good friend to all. Hats were passed in many saloons for donations to his widow. Several thousand dollars in silver and gold were collected to add to the Wells, Fargo award. Sessions's body was carried to its resting place in a stylish black, glass-sided hearse pulled by four plumed horses. Hundreds joined the funeral procession that blocked traffic on C Street as it wound its way to the city cemetery where a graveside service was held.

After Sessions's funeral, Crawford, the young Wells, Fargo agent, sought out Ross and offered him $100 for his rôle in thwarting the hold-up. Embarrassed, and publicity-shy, Ross declined. "First of all, I don't want to become a target for revenge by drawing attention to myself," he told the agent. "But most important, as a government employee, I'm not allowed to accept gifts." This was only partially true, but gave him an excuse for turning down the offer.

Ross took advantage of the lull to catch up on his writing, and to soak his bruised heel in warm water every day to help it mend. His brief rôle as a gun guard for Martin Scrivener was certainly something in the past. He drove himself in a buggy to visit two of the larger, better-run mines for inspection tours. As a precaution, he carried matches and candles, a canteen of water, and his loaded .32 Moore in a shoulder holster. These inspection tours were routine and informative. With the figures of tons of ore mined, numbers of ounces of silver and gold milled, cast into bullion and shipped, Ross was able to form a good idea of the mineral wealth of the Comstock. That's what he'd come here to do. As to the future potential of the region, no one knew. The ledges of metal-bearing ore could give out at any time, and some of the very deepest mines had already begun to experience flooding. To keep the mines dry and producing, more capital would have to be invested in the huge Cornish pumps.

But, for now, in the early summer of 1864, Ross could write up a reasonably accurate report. He was also filling his daily journal with material as valuable to him as silver and gold.

When going about the town, Ross was now more circumspect. He remained acutely aware of everyone around him on the street. Each evening he still met with Martin Scrivener for supper and they shared information like two old friends and confidants. Neither of them could account for the unexpected silence from both Fossett and Tuttle.

"Could be your visit has Fossett cowed," Scrivener said over supper in Barnum's. "Your threat, combined with that arm wound."

"I doubt it," Ross replied. "On the surface, perhaps. But my impression of the man was the same as yours . . . he's sneaky and will look for ways to hurt you or me when we're least expecting it."

"I think Fossett is just a small player in this larger plot involving Tuttle and Holladay. I'm wasting ink on him," the editor said.

"But you can't go one step above and accuse a man like Holladay of criminal activity without at least some sort of proof," Ross said. "With his connections, he could put the *Enterprise* out of business."

Scrivener nodded, sipping his coffee. "Yeah. We gotta be a bit more careful with him. He's ruthless, I hear."

Just then a man in black coat and white shirt approached their table. "Mister Martin McNulty, also known as the Sierra Scrivener?"

Scrivener looked up at this formal greeting. "Yes?"

"My name is S.A. Hedder. I represent Mister Avery Tuttle. He's asked me to deliver the following message to you . . . because you've printed gross insults and lies about him in your newspaper, he has taken the greatest personal affront and demands satisfaction."

Scrivener chuckled at the ridiculously formal manner. "I guess he wants me to print a retraction."

The man slapped Scrivener lightly across the face with a pair of calfskin gloves. "No, sir. You are hereby challenged to meet Mister Tuttle on the field of honor at a place and time to be decided by me and your second. In the Nevada Territory, Navy Colts are the customary weapons."

The color drained from the editor's face. "What?"

"You, sir, have been challenged to a duel. Mister Tuttle assumes you are a gentleman and will accept."

"Tell Tuttle he's out of his mind. He can bring a lawsuit against the paper if he wants to, but dueling is illegal and has gone out of fashion everywhere except in the backward Southern states."

"Mister Tuttle is from South Carolina, sir. I'll tell him you said that."

"Said what?" Sam Clemens had walked up just in time to overhear the last remark.

Scrivener still seemed stunned. "Who . . . or what . . . are you, again?"

The man drew himself up to his full height of at least six feet two. "I'm Spanger Arlo Hedder," he replied. "Known as S.A. Hedder. That's spelled with two Ds."

"I don't give a damn how it's spelled!" Scrivener yelled, springing up. His chair *clattered* backward to the floor. Men at the bar and other diners looked to see what the commotion was about. The editor had fully recovered, and his eyes were blazing. "You can tell Tuttle to stick his dueling pistol in his mouth or anywhere else convenient and blow out what brains he's got. I'm not meeting him to fight any duel!"

Ross had never seen him so angry. He stole a glance at Clemens who'd approached the table in a jocular attitude, but now looked stricken.

"I'll be acting as Mister Tuttle's second in this affair," Hedder repeated, unruffled. "Once you name a second, we can arrange further details." He gave a formal half bow and started to withdraw.

But Clemens jumped in front of him, face reddening. "Hell, Tuttle's so stupid he doesn't even know who wrote those articles!"

Hedder drew himself up to his full height and looked down at the agitated reporter. "Who did, sir?" he asked.

"Well . . . I did . . . if you must know the truth of it." He paused as if he'd gone too far, but wasn't sure how to back out.

"I'm sorry, Mister . . . ?"

"Clemens. Sam Clemens. A reporter for the *Enterprise.*" He hesitated, then recklessly plunged ahead. "I started all this with my editorial pieces about Fossett and later about Tuttle. Tuttle's a damned fraud, trying to sell shares in that worthless Blue Hole Mine. And Fossett got himself shot trying to burn down our newspaper office. A pair of low-down crooks! And I was the one who exposed them. Me! Not him!" He jabbed a finger at Scrivener.

"Is that a fact?" Hedder said with cold skepticism. He glanced at Scrivener as if for confirmation, but the editor never changed expression. "Then I'll see if Mister Tuttle would consider extending his challenge to you, instead."

"You're damned right! Martin Scrivener is too good a man to be dirtying his hands with the likes of Tuttle or Fossett."

Hedder inclined his head slightly and strode away toward the door.

A hush had fallen over the crowd of customers as all heads were turned in the direction of the drama. As soon as the door slammed behind Hedder, spontaneous applause erupted from the spectators.

"Well, Sam," Scrivener said quietly, picking up his overturned chair, "I don't really need anyone to fight my battles, but you've jumped right into the hot chili with this one."

Chapter Fourteen

"Three more hold-ups in two days!" Scrivener said to Ross as they sat in the *Enterprise* office. "And these were successful. Wells, Fargo took some pretty good hits." He leaned back in his chair. "The robbers killed the guard and one of the passengers who resisted being relieved of his watch." He rose from his chair and paced around the desk, looking out the door into the pressroom. "The only reason the driver wasn't shot on this last job was because he saw it coming, poured a half bottle of whiskey over his head, and slumped down in his seat, pretending to be drunk. They left him alone, figuring he was harmless."

"I was told one of the mine owners cast his silver shipment in one big silver ingot weighing nearly three hundred pounds so the robbers couldn't lift it or carry it away on horseback," Ross said.

Scrivener smiled grimly. "Next thing you

know, the road agents will be bringing saws to cut up the ingots, and pack mules to carry off the pieces. They're starting to act as if Wells, Fargo is hauling treasure for their convenience. At least the robbers can't bring a wagon, or they'd have to stick to the roads in the mountains."

"Since that robbery attempt the day I was aboard, these outlaws are gunning down everyone who gets in their way. And they're scouting to ambush the outriders, too. This has become an all-out war."

"The stakes are high . . . ownership of the Pioneer Stage Line. That earns big money."

Ross tipped his straight chair back on two legs and leaned against the office wall. "Any more tips from Angeline Champeaux?"

"Nope. She told Clemens that Tuttle hasn't been back to see her. Probably doesn't want to take a chance on getting drunk again and blabbing everything he knows."

"Or he has other things on his mind . . . like dueling. Since we haven't heard from him or that officious Hedder in the past two days, maybe Tuttle's trying to decide which of you two he wants to take on."

"Speaking of which, Clemens has been wound tighter than an eight-day clock. Haven't had much work out of him since that little scene at Barnum's the other night."

"In spite of what you said, would you go through with a duel?" Ross asked.

Scrivener shook his head. "No. I'm older and wiser now. The public loves duels for entertainment, but they prove nothing. I'm not afraid of Tuttle, if that's what you're asking. As I told you before, I engaged in two affairs of honor in my younger days. Killed a man the first time . . . a young hothead who was obsessed with defending a woman's honor. The second time, I was out-shot and survived with a flesh wound. Could have been killed, but my opponent blooded me and that provided him enough satisfaction." He rolled up the left sleeve of his white shirt to expose a three-inch long scar where no hair grew on his forearm. "I'd say positively that Clemens has never en-gaged in a duel. He's from a border state where differences are still settled that way now and then, but, in my opinion, he's just not the type. Too progressive in his think-ing. Not hidebound by tradition, I'd guess."

"I wasn't going to say anything until circumstances forced me to, but Clemens confided to me earlier he was responsible for getting you into that affray with Fossett. Sam said he planned to challenge Fossett first to keep him from hurting you. He thinks an awful lot of you. But Sam also said he couldn't hit the wall of a privy if he was standing inside it."

"I'm a good pistol shot," Scrivener said reflectively. "Maybe I should coach him, just in case he's the one Tuttle picks."

"Could be Tuttle has dropped the whole notion since you haven't heard anything from him in two days."

Scrivener nodded. "Possibly. I don't know Tuttle, so I can't hazard a guess." He looked at Ross. "You know, it's a helluva thing for you to come into town on business, and wind up taking on other men's troubles."

"Be a mighty lonely world if everyone kept to himself," Ross said.

"I feel I've known you more than a few weeks."

"And I, you."

They grinned at each other.

"You about to wind up your mine inspections?" Scrivener asked.

"Getting close. But I don't have to leave as soon as I'm done."

"Going to stretch that government *per diem?*"

"No. I'll go on my own time and pay my own expenses for a while. I can't just leave on the stage and not find out how all this pans out."

"It might be months or years before there's any resolution."

"Not if I'm any judge."

"Well, hang around as long as you like. I'm certainly glad for your company."

"Thanks."

"Yep. When you're gone, I won't have anybody left to confide in."

"I don't think I've ever seen a man so immune to gold fever as you," Ross said. "And I should know, because I'm that way myself."

Scrivener chuckled. "What are we doing here, then?"

"Observing all these other fools who're silver mad . . . and reporting on them."

"You're right. I'll probably be still sitting here, collecting my fifty dollars a week salary when the mines are played out and most of the town deserted."

"Let's not anticipate old age."

"Sometimes it's good to reflect on the past and anticipate the future . . . just in case the future is a lot shorter."

A knock on the open doorway interrupted.

Ross had a sudden sinking sensation when he looked up to see S.A. Hedder, wearing a black frock coat and white shirt. The man had the appearance of a tall, lean undertaker.

"Where is Mister Clemens?" Hedder asked in answer to Scrivener's inquiring look.

"He'd better be out gathering the news. He has a column to fill," the editor said briskly. "He might be a couple doors down at the Wells, Fargo office, getting the lowdown on that latest hold-up."

"Thank you." The man nodded and backed out the door with a stiff formality.

"Put a scythe in his hands and he'd look like the Grim Reaper," Ross said, mainly to distract the black thoughts he knew were in Scrivener's mind at the moment.

"I was afraid of that," the editor said. "Let's go find Clemens. He's going to need a drink after Hedder issues that challenge." He reached for his coat.

But Clemens was nowhere to be found. They started at the Wells, Fargo office — where the agent said Sam had been earlier — and worked their way along C Street, before discovering him at the bar in the Blind Mule.

The look on his face told Ross what he needed to know.

"Hedder found you, then?" Scrivener said as they approached the bar. Evidently from long habit, the bartender slid a glass and gin bottle in front of the editor.

"Yeah. It's set for tomorrow morning at nine."

"Where?"

"A patch of desert just past the Blue Hole Mine."

"You actually going through with it?" Scrivener asked.

"Not if there's any way I can weasel out."

Scrivener poured himself a drink. "I'm appointing myself your official coach, adviser, trainer . . . and your second if you need one."

"Thanks. It might be your last official function as far as Sam Clemens is concerned . . . unless you plan to be a pall-bearer, too."

"Don't worry about it. If you decide to refuse the challenge, nobody will think the worse of you for it. It's an archaic practice that should be outlawed in any decent society."

"Washoe is *not* a decent society, and it *is* outlawed," Clemens said morosely.

Ross had to turn away to keep his smile from showing.

Scrivener sipped his gin. "While you're trying to make up your mind, let me get my buggy and we'll go out into the desert. I'll show you a few tricks of marksmanship. You can practice a little under the eye of an expert."

"Not feeling up to it at the moment," Clemens said, smoothing his mustache and tipping his beer glass.

"Then we'll go out in the morning an hour beforehand and practice."

"All right," Clemens said without enthusiasm. "Right now, I have to go and write up my piece about that stage robbery."

Ross and Scrivener left Clemens to brood in his beer.

A little before 8:00 the next morning, the three men rode down into a swale of open ground beyond the Blue Hole, where the duel was to take place. It was a desolate piece of desert behind huge mounds of spoil where only a few clumps of sage managed to survive. Tin cans littered the ground and Ross picked up an empty one-gallon molasses bucket. He laid a board across the top of a broken-sided wooden flour barrel and set the molasses can on top. It approximated a short, fat human target.

"All right, I want to check your hand-eye co-ordination," Scrivener said, instructing his reporter to blaze away with his .36 Colt at a distance of twenty paces. For several seconds, the quiet morning air was blasted with the roar of gunfire. True to Clemens's prediction, the lead balls would have been deadly to man or beast standing anywhere except directly behind or directly in front of the shooter.

In the following silence, the roar of gunfire was heard from the gully just beyond the piles of tailings. They looked at each other.

"Sounds like Tuttle's getting in a little practice, too," Scrivener said. "He'll be along directly."

Ross noted Clemens's normally ruddy complexion had taken on a pale hue in the morning light.

The editor produced another loaded cylinder from his pocket and handed it over. "Here. Give me the empty and I'll have Ross reload it."

Clemens broke the pistol apart, removed the spent cylinder, and inserted the freshly charged one.

"Let's try it again. This time, think of the barrel of the gun as your finger. Just point the finger from waist level at the can. Better yet, go for the hogshead beneath it, like that was Tuttle's body."

The Colt erupted three times with the same results.

"Hold it!" Scrivener stepped forward and

took the Colt. "Since this is a duel, and not the usual gunfight, you'll be standing sideways, arm extended, aiming down the barrel." He handed back the revolver. "Cock it, line up the hogshead through the notch in the hammer with the little bead on the end of the barrel."

Clemens, looking frustrated, tried, but missed the flour hogshead by six feet. Arm fully extended, he cocked and fired again. The gun roared and spat a tongue of flame. The slug kicked up dirt ten yards beyond the target.

"Lemme see that thing," Scrivener said, taking the gun from Clemens's hand. "Might have to work on that front sight. I have to aim low with my own Colt to be on target."

The uproar was finally too much for a sage hen hidden in a clump of brush. With a *thrumming* of wings, she flashed upward. Scrivener snapped off a shot as the bird took flight. The hen flopped into the dust, head missing.

Scrivener handed the smoking Colt back to a wide-eyed Clemens.

Just then a one-horse buggy rolled over the rise and Hedder reined to a stop.

"Nice shot, Sam," Scrivener said, indicating the grouse that still thrashed spasmodically forty feet away.

Hedder's mouth opened and closed twice. "Did you . . . the head . . . ?" He looked from the dead bird back to Clemens, who quickly caught on and blew wispy smoke from the end of his weapon. "I'm still a little rusty," he said to Scrivener. Then he turned to the new arrival in the buggy. "Ah . . . Mister Hedder, good to see you. You know Martin Scrivener, I believe. He'll act as my second. We're about ready, but it lacks twenty minutes to the hour yet," he said, shoving the pistol back into its holster.

Without a word, the tall man snapped the reins over the back of his horse, pulled him around, rode over the rise of ground, and disappeared.

Clemens could hardly contain himself until Hedder was out of earshot. Then he whooped and hollered and the three men folded up with laughter.

"As the reputed best shot in Washoe," Clemens gasped, wiping tears of laughter from his eyes, "I'm buying lunch."

CHAPTER FIFTEEN

"Martin, I can't thank you enough," Clemens said, gripping the editor's hand as they stood on the boardwalk in front of the *Enterprise* office at twilight that evening. "You've been like a father to me."

"Sam, why don't you stay? I'm sure we can work this out, somehow," Scrivener said.

Ross was trying to remain inconspicuous several feet away, but was acting as look-out for the approach of the police chief, Amos McClanahan, who was reported to be on his way to arrest Clemens for illegal dueling.

"Maybe it's meant to be," Clemens said, picking up his leather grip and eyeing the stagecoach across the street through the gathering dusk. "I've been here long enough. Just needed something to kick my ass out of town so I can get on with the rest of my life."

The men were silent for a few seconds.

Then Clemens said: "I can't believe that son-of-a-bitch, Tuttle, slipped the word to the authorities I was going to fight a duel with some unknown man this morning. Why in hell would they enforce a law against dueling, when murder goes unsolved every day?"

"This is the territorial governor's doing," Scrivener said. "The new law against dueling hasn't been tested yet, but a conviction for even issuing a challenge carries a two-year prison sentence." He turned to look down the street. "Since your brother Orion used to be the governor's secretary, he was able to buy you a few hours of time. But if you're not out of town on the eight-thirty stage tonight, the police chief, acting for the governor, has been ordered to arrest you."

"What about you? You were my second."

"I know a couple of choice personal tidbits about the governor that will appear in my editorial column if I'm bothered by him or his minions. In the event of my arrest, the associate editor is instructed to remove the editorial from my safe and set it in type. I don't think the governor will risk ruining his political career just to see me go to jail for abetting a duel. Maybe if I sent word to him that I'd run it unless you're allowed to stay, then. . . ."

"No, no. I can't allow you to use your only bargaining chip for me," Clemens said. "You need to save it for something really important. In the meantime, I'm not sticking around to go to prison for something I had no intention of following through with."

"You'll be back, won't you?" Scrivener asked.

"Sure will, after things cool down, or the governor is replaced. But I need to try my luck in San Francisco first."

"If things don't work out, you've always got a job here as long as I'm editor."

"Thanks. Say good bye to Angeline for me, will you? Damn! Wish I'd progressed beyond a brother-sister relationship with her."

The driver slammed one of the stage doors, and climbed to the box.

"I better go," Clemens said. He turned and gripped Ross's hand in silent farewell, then dashed across the street toward the stage, disappearing into the gloom.

A minute later the stage jerked into motion and rattled down the street and disappeared around a corner.

Scrivener let out a sigh. "That's one more thing I have against those bastards at the Blue Hole Mine," he said. "They cost me a good reporter and friend."

"Just in time," Ross said. "Here comes McClanahan." The beefy Irishman came swinging down the sidewalk, unlit cigar jutting from beneath his salt-and-pepper handlebar mustache.

"If he wasn't the law, and a good deal bigger than I am, I'd bust him right in the chops," Scrivener growled.

"A sure way to get thrown in jail, in spite of your hold over the governor."

"I think maybe Fossett and Tuttle cooked up this whole thing about a duel just to get me jailed and out of the way. Then Clemens jumped in and fouled up their plans."

"If that's the case, the challenge would have been issued to you . . . not to Clemens."

"You've got a point." Scrivener shook his head, gnawing at the corner of his mustache.

McClanahan came up, brass buttons on his blue uniform gleaming in the lamplight from the saloon across the street. "Martin, did your man, Clemens, get on that stage that just left?"

"Sure did," Scrivener said through clenched teeth. "Now that we're rid of one more dangerous criminal, you'll be free to turn your law enforcement talents to solving a few of the murders that happen in this town every day."

"Don't be gettin' smart with your mouth," the chief said, "or you'll be eatin' jail grub with it before the day's out."

"Come on, Ross, I need a drink and a good cigar."

Ross joined the editor as he hopped across the street on a series of planks partially sunk in mud. They reached the opposite sidewalk and strode off toward the Blind Mule.

"Well, I wish Sam would've at least stopped to tell me good bye," Angeline said, looking petulant. She moved out of earshot of everyone except Ross and Scrivener.

"He was in a big rush to wind up his affairs," Scrivener explained. "The law was on his tail." He quickly outlined the situation.

"They'd arrest him for taking target practice in the desert?" she asked, arching her lovely brows.

"He was accused of dueling, or planning a duel . . . or something," Scrivener said. "It's a long story. Mostly about politics and vengeance." When Scrivener tried to explain this to her, it sounded completely ridiculous. "He was really upset," Scrivener continued, evidently trying to soften the blow. "He thinks an awful lot of you and was afraid he'd become too emotional if he faced you himself. But he did promise to come back. Said he'd try his luck at newspapering in San Francisco. After nearly two years on the *Enterprise* he felt he was in a rut. This was the spur he needed to move on and seek his fortune."

"Don't make excuses for him," she said, cutting through the sham. "The least he could've done was come by and give me a peck on the cheek."

"He would've liked to do a lot more than that," Ross said, then immediately wished he'd kept his mouth shut.

She heaved a great sigh, nearly popping out of the top of her low-cut dress and distracting Ross, who had to step back and pretend not to notice.

"He was one of my best friends," she lamented. "And one of the few men I could completely trust. I told him all my secrets, and knew he wouldn't repeat them unless I gave him permission."

"I know. We're all going to miss him." Scrivener lowered his voice. "That information about the stage robbery you passed along to him a week ago helped stop the robbers from getting away with it."

She nodded. "I was only trying to help out. I haven't seen Avery Tuttle since."

"He's the one who put the law on Sam."

"I don't think I could stand to look at Tuttle again without spitting in his eye," she said, glancing around, as if she expected to see him in the room. "I'm off duty and don't have an appointment tonight," she said, abruptly changing the subject. "I could sure use a drink."

"I'm buying," Scrivener said.

Angeline ordered a sweet sherry, Scrivener his usual gin, and Ross a beer.

"You don't have to go to work tonight, and I'm buying," the editor said to Ross. "Why don't you order something stronger?"

"In my wild youth, hard liquor had its way with me," Ross said. "We carried on a love affair for a time, but I found out shortly I didn't have the stamina to keep up with it. Old tangle-foot sometimes loosed the tiger in me, sometimes Don Juan, and sometimes the court jester, but I had no control over any of them. Finally got wise enough to break off the affair and I've stuck to beer ever since."

Scrivener nodded. "Not every man can learn from experience. Most of us continue to repeat the same mistakes over and over."

At that moment, in the tack room of a stable located between Virginia City and Carson City, Ben Holladay was convening a meeting with Avery Tuttle and Frank Fossett.

"I'll be brief," Holladay said, turning up the wick of the overhead lamp.

Fossett held his breath, hoping this impromptu meeting didn't concern him directly. At least it wasn't a big inconvenience for him to be called away from a late supper, since he lived only a mile away. Holladay's stable was better than Avery's mansion with all its finery, anyway. The Overland Stage Line connected Virginia City to points east and north. The horses and mules for that line were housed here.

"I want to let you know, after that disastrous hold-up a week or so ago, our boys have pulled off more than a dozen successful robberies of Wells, Fargo coaches. One we hit wasn't carrying anything much, but that's rare. Nearly every coach to or from Washoe west across the mountains has valuable cargo aboard. I make sure some of the treasure is being shipped by my stand-ins." He stood with feet wide spread and hands behind his back. "Wells, Fargo isn't ready to crack yet, but I'm sure they're having to subsidize the Pioneer Stage Line with profits from their banking operation. It won't be long now before they'll be more than happy to accept an offer from me to relieve them of that money-losing line." He looked directly at Tuttle with his beady-eyed stare. "When we met before, that man Ross. . . ."

"Gilbert Ross," Avery said. "The mine inspector."

"Yes, yes. Have you heard any more from him?"

Avery hesitated, then said: "He killed two of your three men who died in that aborted hold-up attempt several days back. He was only a passenger, but he's mighty handy with a gun. The newspapers and Wells, Fargo tried to make a hero of him."

Holladay's face suffused nearly purple in the lamplight. He turned away and silently paced the small room.

"But he's out of the picture now," Tuttle hastened to add. "The *Enterprise* ran a story about Ross's experience down in the Blue Hole, and his claim the mine was salted. But nobody took any note of it. The mine's stock has continued to rise." He expanded his chest, sucking in his paunch. "In fact, we sold two big chunks of stock to British investors."

"I know that," Holladay snapped. He paused. "I've brought in a gunman I call The Enforcer." He paused again to stare at them.

Fossett looked down at his boots. He was

becoming very bored with these dramatic pauses. If the man had something to tell them, why didn't he just come out with it?

"I want you to meet him." He reached for the door latch. "Don't try to talk to him. He's a man of . . . *unusual* personal traits. And he's entirely devoted to me. He'll immediately obey any order I give." A grim smile stretched his lips. "He's more like a trained timber wolf than a man."

Holladay swung open the door and a lean man glided into the room.

Fossett felt a shiver go up his back.

"Gents, this here is Billy Joe Slater."

The newcomer stared blankly at them without acknowledging the introduction in any way. In his left hand he held a hat studded with silver conchos.

Fossett, who was accustomed to judging men at a moment's meeting, saw a man about thirty-five with black hair and brows, well-groomed nails, hands that had probably not done a day's work in years. The upper part of his face appeared wind-burned, but the lower part was pale with a trace of the blue-black shadow of his recently shaved beard. He wore a Colt in a black holster. But it was the eyes that held Fossett's interest. They were flat, dead orbs that looked upon the world with no more animation than if he were some sort of zombie. They seemed to have no intelligence behind them. Except that the eyes were not slitted like a cat's, the man resembled a black panther, trained to kill on command. This impression was enhanced when the lean assassin glided, cat-like, out the door.

"Keep watch outside until we're finished," Holladay said. He latched the door and turned back to them. "He's a deadly marksman with a rifle as well as a Colt. When both guards and drivers begin dying during our hold-ups, Wells, Fargo will have trouble finding good replacements. It won't be long before the Pioneer Line is mine." He reached for the door latch. "That's all for now. I'll get word to you if I need you."

The three men filed out into the darkness.

So, Holladay had a killer attack wolf on a leash, Fossett thought. Slater appeared to have some inhuman quality. Maybe some kind of crazy who'd kill on command. Fossett began to shiver, and hid the fact by easing his injured arm back into its sling. He knew about Tuttle's *faux pas* of bragging to his high-priced prostitute concerning plans to rob the first big shipment — plans that had failed because of his loose talk. Tuttle threatened death to Fossett if he ever told

Holladay. Although the damage was already done, a desperate Tuttle swore he'd never touch another drop of liquor. Instead, he distracted himself with trying to get Martin Scrivener and his reporter, Clemens, in trouble with the law. Fossett wasn't too sure what had happened, but somehow Clemens had been forced to leave town, while Scrivener still occupied the editor's chair, as sassy as ever.

Instead of being afraid of Tuttle, Fossett had taunted him. "You won't be able to do anything to me, if I do tell Holladay," he'd said. "You'll be too busy picking out your burial suit. Hope I'm in your will." He'd laughed in Tuttle's face. The older mine owner's cherubic complexion had suffused a bright red. From that moment on, he and Tuttle had hardly spoken.

Fossett had gradually come to the conclusion that whatever money he was to be paid by Tuttle and Holladay, the risk in continuing to work for them might be too great. It wasn't worth dying for. Yet, as a one-third owner of the fraudulent Blue Hole Mine, he wasn't too sure how to extricate himself from the clutches of these plotters. When he'd first entered into this, he was not averse to taking money under false pretenses, but things had gotten considerably more serious. Armed robbery of hundreds of thousands of dollars, innocent people killed, an assassin hired deliberately to murder stage drivers and guards — he began to wonder where it would all end. Even if he wasn't killed, he could very likely find himself spending the rest of his life in prison, or having his trachea tweaked on the gallows. He was glad he'd eaten supper before he came; he'd have trouble explaining to his wife why he had no appetite.

CHAPTER SIXTEEN

Before dawn the next morning, Jacob Sturm died. The former miner finally succumbed to the silicosis that had ravaged his lungs. Gil Ross found out when he stopped at the boarding house on his way to breakfast in town. He wanted to have a word with Sturm's roommate, John Rucker.

Rucker opened the door to Ross's knock, and stepped back, mutely gesturing at the pale figure on the bunk. Ross had seen the hearse outside, and recognized the lean undertaker, Cyrus Blackstone, who was unrolling a large piece of white canvas and spreading it on a stretcher beside the bed.

"Help me lift him," Blackstone said, and he and Rucker gently moved the body from the bed to the stretcher on the floor.

Ross took a long, last look at the face of a man he'd never known in full vigor of life. The anguished expression was gone; he'd ceased to struggle for breath, and the seamed face with the gray stubble had relaxed in his last sleep.

Ross moved out of the way for Blackstone to wrap the canvas over the ravaged body and fasten it to hooks on the sides of the stretcher. Then the undertaker and Rucker, whose eyes were moist, carried him outside and slid the stretcher into the open back doors of the tall, glass-sided hearse.

"I have two others ahead of him, but I should have his body ready by late this afternoon," Blackstone said to Rucker as he closed and fastened the doors.

Rucker nodded, and went back inside.

"Are you the only undertaker in town?" Ross asked the black-coated man who was swinging up to his high perch on the driver's seat.

"I'm it."

"How do you keep up with all the deaths?"

"Hear tell another man is bringing his practice over from Sacramento. Normally I wouldn't welcome competition, but this time I can hardly wait. If business keeps booming like it's been for the past months, I'm liable to become one of my own customers." He snapped the reins and his team started, turning the corner of the building, drawing the hearse toward the street.

Ross went back inside and found Rucker

sitting on a chair, elbows on knees, head in his hands. Ross put a consoling hand on the man's broad back.

Rucker looked up. "I've known Jake for close onto twelve years. I'm sure gonna miss him. . . ." His voice broke and he stopped.

Ross considered uttering some platitude about the man being relieved from his suffering, but decided against it. Rucker knew all that, and would hear it from others. Theirs was a hard life that didn't make for longevity. "Any news from Union Hall?" he asked.

Rucker nodded. "A strike vote set for tonight."

"A strike vote?"

"Only against the Blue Hole. We've had enough of Tuttle. It won't really be a strike because there's nothing to negotiate. Besides his breaking the contract in regard to working conditions, the mine is worthless and our men know it. We'll quit him cold. He'll have to shut down, because no replacement workers will buck the union."

"Won't that throw a lot of miners out of work?"

Rucker shook his head. "There's a big demand for experienced miners on the Comstock."

Ross silently absorbed this news. When

247

word got out of the union's action, the price of Blue Hole stock would drop to nothing. Tuttle and Fossett might be able to sell out dirt cheap to some speculator who would rake through the tailings, or try to rediscover some ledge or vein that was missed.

Ross drew a deep breath. Virginia City and Gold Hill existed on hope and speculation. Regardless of how much precious metal was actually within these mountains, the whole Washoe area was sustained on delusion. Without imagination and deception, this place would be only a tenth its size.

"You think the outcome of the union vote is a sure thing?" Ross asked.

"No doubt about it. I expect it to be unanimous. The vote is only to make it official."

"Do you mind if I alert Martin Scrivener at the *Enterprise*? He can write an article for tomorrow morning's edition. The paper won't hit the street until a few hours after the vote."

"Good idea," Rucker said. "By the way, I saw that piece a few days ago about what Gunderson did to you in the Blue Hole." He shook his head. "Can't blame you for pulling a gun on a couple of the boys and making them take you to the hoist. Getting lost down there can make a man panic.

Happened to me once when I was younger."

"I wouldn't have shot them."

"Figured as much from what they told me. You fired to miss and scare 'em. You picked up a few salted ore samples, too, which proves what Jake discovered."

"Yeah. The ore is still in Scrivener's office safe. But that revelation didn't do anything except make the stock price rise."

"Probably because the news didn't get beyond Washoe," Rucker said. "I don't know much about the business end of mining, but most of that stock is likely sold in other parts of the country."

"Delusion, trickery, lies," Ross said, "keep it all afloat." He shook his head. "A little truth now and then would be refreshing." He thrust out a hand to Rucker who gripped it. "I'll be on my way, then. I didn't know Jacob Sturm long, but he seemed like a fine, honest man. I'll see you at the funeral."

The miners voted to walk off the job at the Blue Hole, and the mine was deserted two days later when they all attended Jacob Sturm's modest funeral. Ross and Scrivener were there as well. The minister held a moving graveside service that had Ross thinking of his own mortality.

Afterward, he and Scrivener left the cemetery with the dispersing crowd, and walked back to town in the hot June sun. Ross decided he didn't need any morose thoughts on such a beautiful summer day. He inhaled a deep breath of the dry, invigorating air that carried a hint of sage.

"You found any more good arrowheads?" Ross asked to divert his own thinking.

"Haven't had time to do any hunting lately," Scrivener said. "But I need to make time. Life isn't just about work."

"If you don't mind, I'd like to go with you."

"You're welcome. Two pairs of eyes are better than one. Especially since mine are starting to need spectacles."

"Reading too much agate type by lamplight," Ross said. "You know, I'm a pretty fair proofreader. Why don't I come down this evening, and help you. Maybe you can finish early and go home to bed. Then we'll do a little arrowhead scouting tomorrow around midday."

"How much do you charge for your services?" Scrivener asked with a slight smile.

"Only good company."

"You work cheap. Come on down to the office later. If we skip supper, we can probably be out of there by two in the morning."

The wind had begun to pick up. Ross squinted and averted his face from a dust devil cavorting across the sagebrush flat. *"Whew!"*

"About time for one of our famous Washoe zephyrs," Scrivener said, holding onto his hat.

"I remember those from the first time I was here . . . mountains tearing the west wind apart and sending it tumbling down this side like an invisible waterfall. Scatters stuff in every direction."

"Even buildings."

The west wind from the Pacific continued to blow the rest of the day, increasing in velocity, pouring down the eastern slope of the Sierras, tumbling great, heavy globs of air into the valleys below as if it were something that could be seen as well as felt.

"Somehow we've missed the Washoe zephyr since you've been in town," Scrivener remarked as he and Ross stood at the front door of the *Enterprise* office and looked out at the chaos on C Street.

"Zephyr?" Ross said. "Doesn't that word mean a light, gentle breeze?"

"Folks around here are given to irony."

"So I shouldn't be surprised if I see a tin roof, or an iron stove or a mule go flying overhead."

"Exactly."

They stepped back into the doorway as an empty bucket went *clattering* and *banging* along the street. A man's slouch hat flattened itself against the tall glass window of the *Enterprise* office, then was snatched away by a gust and blown under the wheels of a wagon.

"A certain way the wind whips around usually deposits lots of hats in a gulch back of town. After a zephyr, the Digger Indians go down there and harvest as many as they can carry. Their kids show up on the streets wearing two or three at a time. Adults, too."

Everything that wasn't indoors or securely fastened was being shifted to another location. The air was full of handbills ripped from walls and posts; playing cards fluttered like falling leaves. The *clatter* of loose objects punctuated the roar of wind moaning around corners of buildings.

An alert pedestrian dived into the dirt street to avoid a green shutter sailing toward his head. The shutter missed him and struck a draft horse a glancing blow. The startled animal lunged sideways against his harness mate and the two of them, along with the wagon they were hauling, charged up onto the boardwalk, tearing down a support post.

Part of the sidewalk roof collapsed, further spooking the horses that rushed back into the street, heedless of the shouts of the driver.

"A lot of free entertainment," Ross commented as the men retreated to the office to finish their work. The compositors were nearly ready for the corrected proofs.

By the time the two men finished at 12:30 a.m., the wind was a howling fury. What had gone before was only a warm-up.

They carried their hats in their hands as they left the office and started down C Street. There was no such thing as leaning into the wind, or bracing one's feet as the rushing air pushed from behind. The gusts seemed to come from all directions at once, whipping dust into the eyes from a dried-up street. Fine sand stung Ross's face; he held up his hat to shield himself from the buffeting. They made no effort to speak as they struggled toward the Blind Mule for a beer and a snack before heading to their boarding house.

Walking head down, Ross suddenly bumped shoulders with a woman coming the other direction. "S'cuse me, ma'am!" He backed up and looked. "Angeline!" he said, recognizing the beautiful face deep inside the hood of her cape.

"Hello, Gil. 'Evening, Martin."

In spite of the hour, she showed no signs of fatigue, no shadows under the eyes. But then, Ross realized, she'd probably slept a good portion of the day. Like the editor, her work was afternoon and into the night.

"Where're you going?" Scrivener shouted above the roar of the wind.

"Home to my hotel room!"

"Would you like an escort?" the editor offered.

"I don't want to take you gentlemen away from anything important."

"We just finished work. Come on, we'll walk with you."

They all turned and started back in the direction of the newspaper office, one of the men on either side of her.

It was easy for Ross to forget what she did for a living. Where he came from, every female was treated as a lady by the men — if not by many of the disapproving women. In any case, he thought, it wasn't his job to judge anyone. She'd been most valuable in helping prevent the loss of a big shipment of treasure, by alerting Clemens to the information Avery Tuttle had given her.

All three of them had to stop suddenly and turn their backs to a strong gust. A canvas cover tore loose from a wagonload of furniture and went sailing over their heads.

"This wind just wears me out!" Angeline shouted above the uproar.

They were beyond the *Enterprise* office and less than a block from her hotel when they heard a muffled *boom* and felt the ground tremble.

"They must be blasting pretty close to the surface!" Scrivener said.

"That was the noise of thunder from that awning flapping!" Ross said, pointing to the whipping canvas above a store front.

"No, I felt a concussion!" Scrivener said, stopping to look carefully around at the buildings on the street. He bumped Ross's arm and pointed. They stood at the entrance to a narrow alleyway between two buildings. Ross saw smoke drifting from a broken window in the alley. Wind whipped the smoke away as soon as it appeared.

He looked back at the editor. "The Wells, Fargo office!"

"The shutters are closed in front and I can't see any lamplight through the cracks!" Scrivener said, looking up and down the imposing two-story brick structure.

"The office on the ground floor never closes!" Ross finished the thought.

"Let's take a look! Stay here, Angeline!"

the editor said, nudging her up into the doorway of a closed store to shelter her from the worst of the wind.

Not knowing what to expect, but preparing for the worst, Ross pulled his Navy Colt and followed the editor to the front door of the Wells, Fargo office. With the roar of the wind in their ears, they could hear nothing else as they paused by the door. Ross carefully grasped the knob and turned. It was locked.

"Something wrong! Let's try the back door!" Scrivener said.

They eased down the narrow alley to the broken window that was still leaking a little smoke. Ross paused and slid one eye around the edge of the broken pane. Someone was moving inside, but the light was so dim from a lamp on the floor he couldn't make out what was going on. Then his eyes became accustomed to the dimness and he could tell the two big doors of the six-foot safe were standing open. Ross ducked beneath the window and grabbed Scrivener's coattail as the editor was making for the rear of the building. "Lamp's on the floor, I can smell burnt powder and the safe's open!" he said.

"Did you see Agent Crawford?"

"Too dark to make out faces, but there's

more than one man inside! Looks like somebody cleaning out the safe!"

Hugging the wall, they moved a few feet farther. "Only two doors to this place and the front one is locked!" Scrivener said.

"Must be hauling the stuff out the back way where there's no light from the street!"

The wind, deflecting between the buildings, whisked their words away. Scrivener put his mouth close to Ross's ear. "Let's take a look around back! Then send Angeline for the police!"

The Washoe zephyr was blowing over trash barrels, banging shutters, and creating such a cacophony, nothing else could be heard. Flattened to the ground, they wiggled along the gravelly earth to where they could peek between a rain barrel and the corner of the building. A low light emanated from the open back door, illuminating a tall-sided freight wagon, the eight-mule team shuffling nervously in the windstorm. Heavy boxes and bags were being handed out and piled into the wagon. Ross recalled payday at the mines was next week. Crawford usually received shipments of gold and silver coin from San Francisco for the mine supervisors to pay the men in specie.

Was this part of the Holladay operation to cripple Wells, Fargo, or some gang operating independently? Robbing the lone agent in the middle of the night was certainly less risky than stopping a stage on a mountain road and having to contend with armed guards, outriders, and possibly armed passengers. The only risk here was that the Wells, Fargo office was in the middle of town. But someone had wisely waited for the first good Washoe zephyr of the season to roar down the mountains and cover the noise of their blowing the safe.

Ross touched the editor's side to get his attention, then pointed back to the street. Scrivener nodded. Ross would go have Angeline summon the law.

Just as he turned, Ross sensed movement behind him, then smelled a delicious lilac fragrance as Angeline dropped to her knees beside him. "I had to see!" she said breathlessly.

Before he could answer, Ross saw the outlines of two men silhouetted by lights from the street. They were cut off in the alley. A shuttered lantern suddenly flashed. "Hold it right there!"

Ross grabbed Angeline, rolled to his left, and fired at the light. The lantern splattered and went out. Guns roared. Ross felt a bullet burn his left forearm. He fired twice more as fast as he could cock the hammer and pull the trigger. A man went down.

He was vaguely aware of shouts from behind the building and Scrivener's gun roaring beside him. He had a fleeting thought for the safety of Angeline, but it was too late for any of them now. Guns were flashing and bullets hitting wooden walls and throwing up spurts of gravel. A lead slug *whined* off a brick wall. In the uncertain light, Ross could only see bulky figures moving, hear shouts above the wind. He pushed Angeline down against the wall.

Everything was happening at once, but it seemed time had slowed to a crawl, and each movement took a long time. He was on his hands and knees, firing, until his Colt was empty. He dropped it and reached under his coat for his smaller, .32 back-up pistol. Just as he yanked it from his inside pocket, something struck him on the side of the head. He saw an explosion of bright light and then — nothing.

Chapter Seventeen

Ross came close to consciousness — just close enough to feel himself being jostled and rolled on something hard. He was moving but, try as he might, he couldn't break through the upper surface of wakefulness. As if in a dream, he couldn't speak, nor could he move his arms and legs, and slipped back into the void.

What seemed a long time later, he opened his eyes. He was lying on his back in the dark, and was no longer moving. He put a hand to the side of his head and it came away sticky. A knot the size of a walnut had swollen above his temple. He recalled wearing his hat when he'd been struck, so was lucky the hat had taken some of the force from the blow. His head ached.

Where was he? He sniffed the faint odor of old grease. Without moving his head, he cut his eyes to one side and the other, which brought a sharp pain. He listened. No sound except the wind *rattling* and *banging* loose metal somewhere close. He tried rolling onto his side. Waves of nausea swept over him. He lay face down on the smooth, packed dirt that smelled of oil and manure.

He blinked a few times, took a deep breath, and pushed himself to a sitting position. Then he saw a slight movement nearby. Indirect, wavering candlelight revealed two bound figures a few feet away. He crawled closer and saw Martin Scrivener and Angeline Champeaux, both bound with arms at their sides, and gagged. He was relieved they were alive. If they'd been killed, there would have been no need to tie them. Why hadn't he been bound? Probably because he was unconscious. Had they been dumped here? Wherever *here* was. He rubbed a stinging burn on his left forearm. In the dim light he could see a long cut, but didn't recall being shot. But he didn't recall much of anything about that gun battle.

He worked the gags out of their mouths.

"Thank God," Scrivener breathed. "I didn't think you'd ever wake. See to Angeline."

He began to loosen her ropes.

They rubbed their stiffened limbs until circulation was restored and they could stand.

Ross felt muzzy, and couldn't seem to get his thoughts straight. "Where are we?"

With Angeline leaning on his arm, Scrivener walked stiffly to the open door and looked out.

Ross followed. "Appears we're in a building housing the hoisting works of a mine," he said. "You know this place, Martin?"

"No."

Ross pulled a bandanna from his pocket and held it gingerly to the side of his head. "Are either of you hurt?"

"I don't believe I am," she answered, her voice shaking.

"No damage here," Scrivener said. "But I can't imagine why, with all that lead flying."

"I think I hit one," Ross said, speaking low and looking around. "And I'm pretty sure you did, too."

"Did they just leave us here?" Angeline asked.

"If we're lucky, they did," Scrivener said.

"Maybe they knew we couldn't see well enough to recognize anyone."

"Only reason we're still alive."

"But how could they be sure?"

"Someone on the street must have heard all that shooting and yelling," Scrivener said. "Probably went for the law. By now they've likely found the Wells, Fargo office looted."

"What time is it, anyway?" Ross asked.

Scrivener pulled his pocket watch and held it close to his eyes. "Three thirty-five."

"At least two hours until daylight," Ross said. "If you can walk, let's get out of here and see if we can find our way back to town. Gold Hill or Virginia City must be close by."

"Nice of them to leave us a candle," Angelina said, pulling the thick candle loose from the melted wax where it was stuck near a windlass. There was no horse or mule to run the windlass. The whole place gave off the stale air of abandonment.

"I wouldn't be for taking that candle anywhere just yet, missy," a strange voice said from the shadows beyond the platform.

Angeline jumped with a little cry, nearly dropping the candle. A chill ran up Ross's back to the base of his neck and he automatically reached for his Colt, which wasn't there. His heart began to pound and, with it, his head. A hand inside his coat confirmed that his .32 was gone as well.

He heard the ratcheting of a lever-action rifle being cocked. A man stepped into the candlelight. The illumination showed his face beneath the hat brim, and it was nobody Ross knew. If either of the others recognized him, they said nothing. The man was in need of a shave, a bath, and a square meal was Ross's quick assessment. A hireling, no doubt.

A silence ensued, during which Ross felt his head throbbing. The cut had ceased to bleed, but he felt sure the knot on his head was large enough to be seen through his hair.

"We'll be heading back to town," Scrivener said, apparently to break the tension of the silence as much as anything.

"No. My orders are to hold you here until the others come back." He stepped to the empty door frame and looked out into the darkness.

"If you haven't already collected your share, what makes you think they're *coming* back?" Ross asked, taking a chance he might guess right.

"I've been paid," the man said shortly.

Angeline dripped hot wax on the hard packed earth and stuck the candle in it. Lacking any chairs or boxes to sit on, all three sat down on the ground to wait. The man with the rifle yawned and leaned against the windlass, looking bored and sleepy. He didn't seem to mind if they talked among themselves. Besides, the *rat-*

tling of the tin building hid their words from him.

"I think this might be the Dead Broke Mine," Scrivener said. "It's a played-out mine the owners abandoned a few months back."

"Appropriate name," Ross said.

"Actually there's probably rich ore under all the mountains in this vicinity, but the owners just ran out of money before they tapped into a ledge, so they had to give it up when they couldn't find investors."

An endless thirty minutes crawled by. The wind buffeted the hoisting works housing, rattling the loose tin siding. It created such a din that, at first, Ross didn't hear the approaching hoof beats. A horse snorted, and the next second three men entered on foot, single file through the empty doorway. Frank Fossett led the parade, his arm still wrapped, but out of the sling. Then came blond, rosy-cheeked Avery Tuttle. He was followed by a third man — a lean stranger who moved with an easy, cat-like grace, and stationed himself to one side, arms folded, looking bored. The only person missing was Ben Holladay. But the big boss would never dirty his hands on the small details of his grand scheme, although he must have known what was going on. He was the brains, the power, and the money behind it all.

"We brought you a spare horse," Tuttle said to the guard with the rifle. "Git!"

The guard didn't need a second invitation. He hustled out the door into the night and Ross heard him ride away.

Tuttle opened two of the shutters on the lantern he carried, and turned up the wick. Wherever they were, apparently he was not afraid of a light brighter than a candle being seen from the outside.

Ross and Scrivener had been disarmed. Whatever was about to happen, Ross would prefer firearms were involved, rather than the mine they were standing atop of. Just then a big, bearded man appeared in the doorway and moved forward into the light.

"Ah, Mister Holladay," Tuttle said in a deferential tone.

"I'll get to the point," Holladay said, taking charge. "We'll have a little trial right here." He removed his stylish gray Stetson and stepped forward, still wearing his long riding duster. A diamond ring on his little finger sparkled in the lantern light. "You've been accused by the prosecuting attorney of attempting to wreck our operation tonight when you came on the scene at the wrong time. It was fortunate you fell into our hands, although you *did* shoot and wound three of my men. We couldn't just kill you and leave your bodies in that alley. That would have created too much of a stir, even in a town that has at least one or two dead men for breakfast every day, including Sunday." He paused to smile at his own wit. "Mister Gilbert Ross, government mine inspector, stands accused of trying to ruin the reputation of the Blue Hole Mine and discredit me, the owner. Not only that, but he shot and killed two of my men while they were attempting to remove treasure from a Wells, Fargo stagecoach. Not satisfied with this shooting, he went to Gold Hill and threatened Frank Fossett with bodily harm." He turned to Scrivener. "Martin McNulty, also known as the Sierra Scrivener, has been a thorn in my side for some time now, writing scurrilous editorials, trying to blacken Mister Fossett's reputation. And now one or both of you somehow convinced the miners' union to quit the Blue Hole . . . in effect, putting that mine out of business, and stealing money from us." He paused and smiled like a cat that has finally captured an elusive mouse. "And last, but far from least, my dear Angeline Champeaux . . . what can I say about you? You and Mister Tuttle were intimate. Regardless of the fact you were more interested in his money than in him, he trusted you. What passes between a man and his mistress should remain sacrosanct, information as privileged as that between a lawyer and his client. . . ."

"I'm *not* his mistress!" Her voice was low and venomous.

"Well . . . a rose by any other name. . . ."

"If you want to call me something, just say I was his high-priced prostitute!" she spat, her cheeks flaming.

"Regardless, my dear," Holladay went on calmly, "you betrayed our secrets to these men, who were instrumental in thwarting our attempt to take a large Wells, Fargo treasure shipment. And your betrayal cost the lives of two of my men." He paused and looked at them, one at a time. "The inspector, the editor, and the beautiful woman. What say you, gentlemen of the jury?" He threw out an arm to an imaginary twelve. "Guilty as charged?"

"Guilty!" Tuttle proclaimed.

"So be it. Now, in my rôle as judge, I must devise a sentence. Of course it will be death. But death can come in many forms. And you three have earned the right to die in a most prolonged and terror-stricken way . . . so that you will have a few hours to meditate on your sins as you pass from this world."

Ross glanced at the lean man in black with a tied-down holster.

"You haven't met Billy Joe Slater," Holladay said, following Ross's gaze. "He's quicker and deadlier than a rattler, in case you have ideas of escaping."

Slater wore a pokerface, black eyes dead in the lantern light. Evidently he was here as an enforcer, as a sergeant-at-arms to make sure everything went as planned.

Angeline wasn't about to take this lying down. As tired and frazzled as she was beginning to look, she loosed a barrage of invective at Avery Tuttle, damning him, all his relatives, and all of his associates to an everlasting, fiery, rotting hell.

In spite of their plight, Ross found himself fascinated by the articulate inventiveness and force of this vituperation. He stole a glance at Frank Fossett. He had the air of a disinterested bystander. Of their four captors, Tuttle and Holladay were the only ones who showed any animation. Perhaps if Angeline could distract them long enough, she'd create an opportunity for Ross to make a break. Holladay had something very fiendish in mind for the three of them, and Ross had no desire to find out first hand what it was.

From beneath half-closed eyelids Ross studied Slater, who was standing closest to him. Would he have a chance to tackle the man and clamp his gun arm to prevent him from drawing? If he missed, it would be all over. But maybe being shot was better than whatever awaited them. If he could somehow communicate his intention to the other two. . . . A good whack on Fossett's injured arm would likely put him out of action in a fight. Tuttle probably had a gun under his duster, but wasn't a good physical specimen when it came to rough-and-tumble. If Scrivener could throw a hard punch at that soft paunch. . . . But Ross knew he couldn't start anything on his own, and risk all their lives. And he couldn't alert the others about his intent.

Angeline finally ran down and paused to catch her breath. In the sudden silence, the tireless Washoe zephyr continued to rattle the tin panels and a few breezes found their way through the cracks to blow the candle, causing wavering shadows. The lantern continued to burn with a steady flame, emphasizing the lines and hollows in several tired faces. The dawn couldn't be more than an hour away.

"Are you finished?" Holladay asked in a calm voice. "Then let the record show that one of the defendants testified on her own behalf."

She caught the would-be judge eyeing her low-cut dress and she pulled the light cape around herself, glaring at him.

"Now, if there is no other business, it's time to carry out the sentence," Holladay declared, rubbing his hands together. He bowed with mock courtesy, and handed Angeline the lighted candle he retrieved from the floor. "Miss Champeaux, I believe it's customary for ladies to go first. If you'll just step this way. . . . Hold your candle so you can see . . . there, now, just step back onto the first rung of that ladder and start down the shaft. It would be much easier and quicker if we could lower all of you in the bucket . . . especially since we've all had a tiring night. But you see we have no horse or mule to work the whim." He did a good job of appearing distressed.

"Why don't you give us that lantern?" Scrivener asked. "This candle might go out."

"Then you can relight it," Holladay replied with a harsh laugh. "We need the lantern, and you don't. The candle is expendable. You might last a little longer than it will."

Ross again looked for a chance to jump Slater. But the smooth gunfighter now had his Colt in hand, pointed their way. There was no chance of escape.

Ross felt a twinge of panic as he climbed down the rickety ladder, shaking with the weight of the other two below him. His worst nightmare was coming true. They were being abandoned to die in an empty mine, hundreds of feet below the surface — to suffocate, to starve, to die of thirst, to be asphyxiated by poison gas, to be crushed by a cave-in, their bodies gnawed by hundreds of rats that infested these dark tunnels.

He prayed silently for a way out. He wanted to rush back up the ladder toward the door so he'd be gunned down. At least it would end quickly. But he had second thoughts about committing suicide when he looked up to see the black muzzle of the Colt in Slater's hand three feet away and pointed right at his head. He wouldn't give them the satisfaction. There had to be another way. And he would find it — or die.

CHAPTER EIGHTEEN

The ladders were in surprisingly good condition for having been neglected for several months. The first one stretched to a rock landing, fifty feet below where the three met and huddled.

A lantern flashed its light down the shaft. "Keep going!" Holladay's voice said. In the hollow silence, they heard the double *click* of his cocking revolver.

They descended another ladder that took them down forty more feet, Ross estimated. Again they stopped, hoping this was as far as they'd be forced to go.

The lighted square at the top of the shaft was blocked as a man began to descend the ladder after them. It was the rotund figure of Avery Tuttle. He stopped at the first landing and yelled down: "All the way to the bottom of the shaft!"

"Are you gong to shoot us if we don't?" Ross yelled back.

"Just drop a few rocks on your heads," he answered.

They started downward. Four more ladders brought them to the bottom of the hoisting shaft nearly three hundred feet below the surface. A point of light flared far above, like someone lighting a match for a smoke.

"What's he doing?" Scrivener asked, looking up.

Before either of them could guess, the pinpoint of light came spiraling down toward them.

"Look out!" Ross cried, pushing them toward the mouth of an intersecting tunnel.

A tight bundle a foot square landed with a thump where they'd been standing.

"Maybe they decided to leave us some food," Angeline said.

Ross cautiously moved to pick it up. A hissing stopped him. He saw the sputtering fuse smoking only two inches from the package — too late to dive and snuff it out.

"Back! It's going to blow!" He only had time to shove them several yards into the tunnel beyond a bracing timber before the tightly bound pack of black powder exploded. The concussion knocked them into a pile atop each other. It was a deep-throated *boom,* louder because it was not imbedded in rock. Smoke and dust boiled into the tunnel; chips of rock sprayed the walls like buckshot. The protective timber leaned drunkenly away from the wall and toppled over.

Ross lay, face to the floor, in total blackness, breathing what air was left.

"Angeline . . . you hurt?" he managed to gasp.

"Don't think so," came her choking voice from under him.

He rolled over, eyes burning. "Martin?"

"I'm all right. Go back and see if the shaft is blocked," the editor said. "Where's the candle?" The darkness was total.

"Here . . ." Angeline said. "In my hand."

Ross heard a match rake against the wall, and Scrivener took the candle from her hand and lighted it. The air was filled with dust and smoke. Angeline's eyes were wide with fear.

Ross took the candle and went back to the shaft. Broken rock was piled to within a foot of the top of the tunnel they occupied. He plowed up the loose pile and held the candle closer to the hole. Most of the rocks were the size of his head or smaller. With the tunnel not completely blocked, they could probably dig their way out. It wouldn't take much to enlarge the opening so they could squeeze through.

He reported his findings to the others.

"We'd best be quiet until they leave," Scrivener whispered, "or they're liable to drop another pack of Giant Powder down to finish the job."

They sat down to wait, leaning against the rough wall with the candle on the floor between them. The dust gradually settled, and the sweat began to dry on Ross. None of them spoke, as if afraid voices could be heard through the small opening in the rocks and all the way up the hollow shaft. But mostly a depressive atmosphere had settled on them. Ross realized this and determined to do something about lifting their spirits.

Finally Ross took the candle and climbed the pile again. He carefully moved a few rocks from the top so he could thrust his head and shoulders through. Twisting onto his back, he tried to see up the hoisting shaft, but everything was black. Either it was still night and their captors gone, or they'd covered the opening at the top.

He came back and reported his finding. "While we wait for daylight, let's explore this tunnel," he said, more to distract their brooding than for any hope of finding a way out. "If we don't go into any cross-cuts or branches, we can find our way back."

Scrivener stood and helped Angeline to her feet. Ross led the way with the lighted candle. The air was fetid, and getting warmer as the tunnel sloped downward. But there was enough oxygen for the candle to burn brightly.

Ross counted his paces. At three hundred he slowed. They'd passed two cross-cut tunnels, and paused to peer into them a few feet with the light, but didn't enter. "Unless we had some way of finding our way back, we'd better not chance getting lost. That main shaft we came down is still our best hope of getting out," Ross said.

"Wonder why they didn't just kill us outright and dump our bodies down here?" Scrivener said.

"Slater would have done it in a second if Holladay had given the word," Ross said, thinking of the blank-eyed killer. "But Holladay likes to be dramatic. Maybe he doesn't have the stomach for cold-blooded murder."

"I think he just wants us to suffer before we die," Scrivener said. "And he can be a great distance away before we finally check out."

The farther they went, the fouler the air became. There were no blowers above, forcing fresh air down the passageways. The candle flame began to burn lower.

"I feel like I'm suffocating," Angeline finally said. "Let's go back. There's no way out in this direction."

"She's right," the editor said. "We'd feel some kind of draft of fresh air if this led to any opening on the surface."

They retraced their steps, Ross carrying the candle and trying to estimate how long it would last.

When they came to within fifty yards of the main shaft, they encountered a cross-cut tunnel. Scrivener stopped. "I feel some cooler air here. Let's explore it."

Ross consented, but had misgivings. The tunnel was smaller and shored up with heavy timbers. Apparently, it'd been long abandoned. The mountain was reclaiming its empty spaces. Support timbers were splintering and bowing from the incessant pressure of millions of tons of rock and earth settling. Fifty yards inside, the air became moist. Algae sprouted on the rotting timbers and the atmosphere was dank and smelled of mold. The cooler air Scrivener detected was due to water tricking from the seams of rock and coursing down the rough walls to collect in a stream on the floor, continuing to flow in the direction they were headed. Only then did Ross realize how thirsty he was.

"Oh, my! I can get a drink and wash my face!" Angeline exclaimed, putting her hand under a stream of water dribbling off a ledge.

They took turns drinking their fill and rinsing the dust from their faces and hands. As refreshing as it was, the water had a strange taste, which Ross didn't remark on. But he thought of the arsenic it probably contained, like much of the drinking water in the town above. It was diluted enough to cause only gastric upsets, rather than death. In any case, they might not live long enough to feel the ill effects of any contamination.

Even though the tunnel trended downward, they were drawn to explore it farther, since the air was cooler. The splintered and sagging overhead timbers were festooned with broad, slimy curtains of fungi, which they ducked under, or brushed aside as they went. Long, squirming ropes of the stuff hung down, twisted into fantastic shapes like the horns of a ram. Monstrous mushrooms of fungi bulged from moisture-filled cracks in the vertical braces.

"Listen!" Scrivener held up his hand for silence and they paused, listening intently. Only the far-off dripping of water and the incongruous ticking of the editor's watch could be heard in the silence. "Thought I heard something that sounded like voices," he said.

"Maybe the voices of miners killed down here," Angeline uttered in a hushed tone. "Like spirits of the dead that walk abroad in the New Orleans cemetery when the moon is full. Bodies are boxed above ground there because the soil is too wet to bury them."

Her brown eyes were wide and solemn in the wavering candlelight.

"Thought I heard something," Scrivener said. "Must've been mistaken. If only this were a working mine, we might have a chance of finding some miners. But. . . ."

"We'll get out of here," Ross interrupted. "If we've seen everything there is to see, let's go back."

"Wait," Scrivener said. "When an ore vein or ledge is located, miners tunnel nearby at an angle to come below it. That way they can blast and cut upward, so the rock will fall down where they can scoop it into ore cars. A lot less lifting that way. They take advantage of gravity when they can. If we keep on this way, we should come to a big cavern where the ore has been blasted out and hauled away."

"Lead on," Ross said, handing him the candle.

Ten more minutes brought them to what might have been a large, airy cavern, only to find it caved in nearly to the ceiling.

"Let's go back," Angeline said, her voice drooping with discouragement. "This is too scary. I'm feeling faint."

Without a word, they retraced their steps until they came to the main drift and turned right for fifty paces to where the blast had partially blocked the tunnel.

Ross and Scrivener busied themselves clawing at the pile, raking rocks backward and enlarging the opening until it was big enough for them to crawl through on hands and knees.

Ross went first and reached back for the candle the editor handed across the pile. His heart sank. The ladder they'd descended had been torn away by the blast to a height of thirty feet — far out of reach. And the vertical walls, although rough, provided no hand or footholds to climb. Hundreds of feet up, gray daylight illuminated the square opening at the top of the shaft. He usually rejoiced with the coming of every day. But now it was only a fact he noted and passed along to the others. Daylight or dark — neither had any significance to them. The thick candle he held could probably last another twelve hours, he estimated. And then they'd be in blackness for whatever time they had remaining. Would it be days of starvation? Would they go mad first? He felt a sinking sensation in his stomach. He couldn't bring himself to voice the questions he knew were in the minds of his two companions. Had anyone missed them? Was anyone looking for them? How would they know where to look? The obvious answers were too discouraging even to think about, much less discuss.

One thing he did know, and that was he had to keep his mind busy. The best way to do that was to look for a way out while they were still reasonably fresh and strong. Mining practices on the Comstock were well known to Scrivener, and he would pick the brain of the editor for his knowledge of which of these tunnels, if any, could possibly lead to the outside.

While Ross was ruminating, Angeline and Scrivener crawled through the opening over the pile of rocks and stood beside him at the bottom of the hoisting shaft. They sat on the floor to rest and Ross began by questioning the editor about the probable design and layout of this mine.

"If we're in the Dead Broke, I can't say

for certain, since I'm not familiar with this particular mine. From what we've already seen, the square set timbering wasn't used in the upper works where we are now. Needed more in the lower levels because of the weight of the rock above. Also, where we've explored so far is the older portion, abandoned before square-set timbering became the norm."

"Where can we go to try for a way out before our candle is used up?"

Scrivener thought for a long minute or two, turning his head this way and that, as if trying to orient his mental picture. Finally he said: "Several of the mines in the region have shafts dug into the lower levels at an angle of about forty-five degrees or less. Ore is loaded into small ore cars called giraffes on rails that are winched up to a vertical shaft where the ore's transferred to big buckets for hoisting to the surface."

"Then an inclined tunnel would terminate right here at the main shaft?"

"Possibly, but I don't see any here. Could be there's more than one vertical hoisting shaft."

"How would finding one of these inclined shafts help us?"

"Depending on how close the outside surface of the mountain was, the inclined tunnel might not connect to the vertical shaft at all, but rather would angle all the way to the outside, usually on the flank of the mountain, and the giraffes hauled out that way. It saves having to transfer the ore once again to the buckets for hoisting straight up."

"I see. . . ." Ross looked from one to the other. "It's a long shot, but sounds as if finding one of those inclined tunnels might be our only chance. What do both of you think?"

Angeline shook her head. "I'm totally out of my element here. It's up to you two. I know nothing about mines."

"I might be totally wrong, but I think that's probably our best hope," Scrivener said. "But we need to find one that goes to the outside, and doesn't terminate in a vertical shaft. To do that from where we are, I think we'll have to descend to a lower level. For ventilation and communication, miners dig winzes which connect one level to another. If we can find one of those, it'll be a quicker way to go deeper in hopes of finding an inclined tunnel."

"If both of you are agreeable, let's get to it. We're wasting candlelight sitting here."

This time, instead of crawling back through the hole over the collapsed pile, they decided to try the tunnel leading off the opposite side of the vertical shaft. Scrivener's sense of direction told them it led toward the east side of the mountain. Tracks for ore cars had been laid in this tunnel and soon curved to the right and began to slope gently downward, apparently following some long-gone vein of ore. They walked more than five hundred paces before Ross lost count, and they stopped to rest.

Using the angle of the grade, Ross calculated they'd now descended more than six hundred feet beneath the surface where they'd first entered the mine. The air grew stagnant, the flame smaller. At a brief rest stop, Ross said: "How many matches do you have?"

Scrivener fished the stick matches from his vest pocket. "Seven."

"Why don't you give us two each and keep the other three. Then, if something unexpected happens, any of us will have the means to light the candle."

"Good idea." Scrivener divided the supply.

They moved on. The candle continued to burn, low and slow. It would now last longer, but all three of them were also having slightly more difficulty breathing, and had to pause more often to rest in the warmer atmosphere.

Down and down they went. "Maybe this is the angled tunnel," Ross said, breaking into a silence of scuffing feet and harsh breathing. "It does have tracks in it for the giraffes to run on."

"I . . . don't think so," Scrivener panted. "An angled tunnel would not curve like this . . . and it would be a little steeper."

The deeper they went, the hotter the air became, until they had to shed their coats, vests, and shirts. Angeline dropped her cape and left it. Her low-cut, sleeveless dress was tattered and streaked with dirt. Deeper into the earth and closer to Dante's hell, Ross thought. He'd stopped counting his paces, but they were at least one thousand to twelve hundred feet down and the temperature was over a hundred degrees. Steaming hot water was oozing from crevices in the walls, and the whole atmosphere began to feel like a Turkish bath. Sweat streamed down their faces and necks and chests, soaking their clothing. Their skin, in the yellow light, shone like it was oiled. Breathing became more difficult even though they were on a downgrade. Apparently this led nowhere, and Ross was about to suggest they return, when Scrivener called: "There!"

"What?"

The editor held up the candle. "See . . . a connecting passage up ahead."

They moved on through the moist heat of rising vapor.

"An intersecting tunnel," Scrivener said, moving into it and holding the candle high. "This is one of those angled tunnels!" he exclaimed, sounding more excited than he'd been since their ordeal began.

Ross and Angeline crowded up to look over his shoulder.

"See? It runs along level for a few yards, then angles up."

"Oh, no!" Ross groaned.

"What's wrong?"

"That gray mud, or clay, is blocking the way."

The three crept forward to where the tunnel was overflowed to a depth of more than two feet by what appeared to be molten lava.

"What's this stuff?" Angeline asked.

"At these depths, the heat and the moisture create a viscous clay that oozes into any open spaces," the editor said. "When the mine was active, the miners had to keep cutting the stuff away as it continually invaded the tunnels they'd just dug out."

"It's stayed hellishly hot," Ross observed. "Any way we can cross it without burning ourselves?"

"It's still thick and glutinous underneath, and would take your skin off nearly as quick as live steam," Scrivener said. "But the surface has cooled a little," he said, carefully touching the mass with a fingertip.

"It's like hot quicksand, then," Angeline said. "It won't hold our weight, and, if we sink down, we'll be scalded."

"It's only about ten feet wide," Scrivener said. "See if you can find a plank to lay across it."

A quick search proved fruitless.

"Here's a twelve-by-twelve upright that's partially rotted," Ross said. "If we can kick it down, that might work."

They pushed and pulled and kicked at it, desperation lending strength to their efforts. All the while, the candle continued to burn, dwindling like an hourglass, shrinking like their hopes.

"Damned thing's wedged tighter than it looks!" Ross gasped, sweat stinging his eyes.

"Yeah, they really cleaned up in this mine when they quit," Scrivener said. "No broken picks or shovels left behind to use as tools. Wish we could wrench up one of these iron rails to use as a pry bar."

A vicious kick finally dislodged the post and it toppled over, followed by several cubic yards of the ceiling that collapsed in a billowing heap. The men leaped back just in time to keep from being crushed.

"Guess that post was holding up more than I thought."

Ross and Scrivener hoisted each end of the heavy timber, lugged it a few feet, and stood it on end at the edge of the amorphous mass of steaming clay. They let it fall across the crusted ooze. It sank a few inches, then stopped.

"I'll try it first," Ross volunteered. "If it'll hold my weight, it'll hold yours."

He hopped up onto the end of the beam and lightly cat-walked his way to the other end and dropped off. "It's good," he said, "Wide enough to keep your balance, too."

"Angeline, rip a foot of material off the bottom of that dress," Scrivener said, "so you won't step on it. Use your arms for balance."

She sat on the floor and managed to tear a ragged strip off the bottom of the long dress.

"*Whew,* that's cooler, too," she said, standing up in her high-buttoned shoes with thick, elevated heels. She scampered across with no trouble. "Just like crossing a creek on a log when I was a girl." She laughed. Her lilting voice was the happiest thing Ross had heard since they were forced into this trap.

Scrivener made it only after he'd nearly overbalanced, but managed to leap off at the other end, Ross catching him.

They looked up the slope of tunnel. "Well, it's this or nothing," Ross said, taking the candle from Angeline. "I'd guess we have no more than five hours of light. No time to go back, even if we wanted to. At least, we're headed in the right direction . . . up."

He fastened his eyes on the outer edge of the circle of light and started forward, leading them. The inclined plane made walking tiring. Their breathing in the fetid air became more labored. Ross's legs began to ache. Finally he paused. "How long we been down here, Martin?"

Scrivener consulted his watch. "*Hmmm . . .* my watch stopped. Must've banged it on something."

"I'm thirsty and hungry," Angeline said, slumping to the floor.

Ross hunkered next to her, afraid if he sat down, he'd have trouble getting up.

The editor leaned against the wall. "We might find some water up above," he said. "Water will take away the hunger pangs for a while. And we can live a lot longer without food than we can without water."

Ross pulled Angeline to her feet and they

plodded on.

After a time, Ross fell into a dull routine where he thought of nothing beyond placing one foot ahead of the other — no vision of the future or the past, focused on one goal only, and that was to reach the end of this tunnel, and hopefully the real world above.

"Seems a lot farther up than it was down," Ross panted.

"You forget we might be already past the level of the bottom of that hoisting shaft where we started," Scrivener said. "And we're walking uphill now. We could be angling toward another exit on the flank or shoulder of the mountain."

Ross had no way of knowing how long they'd walked, but they finally all reached the point of exhaustion, their candle burning dangerously low.

"Let's stop and rest for a while," Scrivener said, panting. "I just want to lie down and close my eyes for a bit."

"Then we should douse our light to save the candle," Ross said. He knew their fatigue was brought on, in part, by the bad air.

"We'll sleep for a few hours, then go on," Scrivener added.

Once they were settled more or less comfortably on the floor, Ross said: "Here goes the light." He snuffed the candle and nearly caught his breath at the sooty blackness that seemed to smother them. He took several deep breaths just to assure himself they were surrounded by air. Then he rolled up the shirt and jacket he'd been carrying and made a pillow for Angeline to keep her head off the rocky floor.

Ross's fatigue and lack of proper oxygen drugged him into a sleep within a few minutes. But, in that few minutes before oblivion overtook him, he heard an eerie creaking in the distance. Except that he was stationary, he could have been hearing the creaking and groaning of a ship's timbers as it wallowed in a windless seaway. That sound was etched in his memory from the months-long voyage around Cape Horn on his way West. Ross attached no significance to the sound as he slid into an exhausted, dreamless sleep.

A piercing scream wrenched him awake. He jerked upright, instantly alert. "Angeline! What's wrong?" Had she lapsed into madness?

"Light the candle! Something alive just ran over my face!"

"Martin!"

"I'm here. You have the candle."

Ross pulled out a match and struck it on the wall, but it didn't light. "Damn!" He felt of the match. The head was soft and crumbly.

"Oh, my God, there it is again," she whimpered, hysteria in her voice.

"Martin, see if you have a dry match."

While the editor fumbled for a light, Ross heard tiny squeaks and scratchings and felt something brush past his pants legs.

"Rats!" he said, a shiver going up his back. "Don't worry, Angeline. Stand over here by me. They won't hurt you." He reached out in the blackness and pulled her close between himself and the wall.

Scrivener muttered a curse under his breath. "All three of mine are too damp to light. Must've been that steamy heat back yonder."

They tried one of Angeline's matches with the same result. "Be careful not to rub the head off the one or two we have left. Maybe they'll dry out later."

Even in total darkness, it was good to have company, knowing two friends were close by, sharing the fear.

Once again came the sound of timbers creaking and groaning, this time louder than before. A loud *crack* startled them. Was someone else down here? Maybe searchers trying to signal them?

"Was that a gunshot?" Angeline asked.

"The mountain is settling, stressing the support timbers," Ross replied. "Nothing to get alarmed about. But that loud popping worries me. That was one of those big timbers breaking."

"Oh."

Every few seconds, the timbers shrieked and groaned as they were squeezed and bent by the overpowering earth.

"Gil!" Scrivener said in a low, urgent voice.

"What?"

"Those rats are all running in the same direction . . . uphill. They can sense a cave-in. Let's go with them!"

"I'll lead," Ross said. "Single file. Angeline, hang onto my belt. Martin, you bring up the rear and grip her hand so we stay together. Run as fast as you can. If you *have* to stop . . . then yell."

She grabbed his belt with one hand.

"Ready, Martin?"

"Go!"

Ross sprinted ahead. For the first few steps, until they got into rhythm, they stumbled on each other's heels. Then Ross settled into guessing where the ore car rails were, and tried to step between them. The warm, foul air filled with a chorus of high-pitched squeaking. Hundreds of tiny nails skittered along the floor as swarms of unseen rodents darted past them.

"Oh!" Angeline shrieked. "One of those rats clawed my bare leg!"

"Keep running!" Ross panted.

Now and then his own foot came down on a soft body and his ankle rolled, nearly throwing him against the wall. The rats were in a panic and would bite at anything, but he ignored them and concentrated on running. Angeline's drag on his belt, and the added strain of Martin holding onto her, made Ross feel he was pulling a train all by himself. Like running in a nightmare, he couldn't seem to move his legs fast enough. His lungs began to burn; his breath whistled between his teeth.

Somewhere behind, timbers screeched in their death agony. A hollow *boom,* like distant artillery, echoed up the passageway. Then began a low growl that grew louder by the second until it was a long, continuous ripping thunder. The tunnel was collapsing on itself. A rush of heated wind swept over them — the hot breath of a pursuing hell they couldn't outrun.

CHAPTER NINETEEN

"Run!" Ross shouted. One last desperate dash for life was all that remained. They let go of each other and sprinted for their lives. In the blackness, Ross had been conscious of tripping or turning an ankle on the rails in the floor. Now, he ran flat out, knowing only that he must outdistance the horror behind him. They knew what that ripping thunder meant, and it had to stop caving before it reached them or they'd be buried like three ants.

Long seconds dragged by and Ross increased his lung-straining effort, aware of the other two close on his heels. Angeline screamed. Ross heard it above the thunder and slowed to help. He fumbled for her in the dark where she'd fallen, and dragged her to her feet. Scrivener collided with them and went down.

"Grab her arm!" Ross yelled.

The men seized her from either side and

propelled her forward, dragging her faster than she could run in the high-heeled button shoes. No longer could Ross hear the squealing rats above the ground-shaking thunder closing on them. He ricocheted off one of the vertical timbers in the narrow tunnel, and tried to move a little ahead of Angeline to miss the next obstruction.

"We can't . . . make it!" she wailed.

"Run!"

Sobbing for air, she wind-milled her legs ever faster to keep up with her body.

Ross's eyes were wide open, but saw nothing but blackness. The dusty, smothering presence grew closer and louder, crashing and thundering, preparing to swallow them. His lungs burned and he began to see spots before his eyes. He blinked and they went out. He looked and saw it was really there — one spot, bouncing in his vision, making it look like two or three. A gray spot of light some distance ahead.

"Look!" he shouted, with no breath for more words.

Adrenaline gave him a surge of energy and his feet flew over the ground, lightening Angeline's weight. He smelled no freshness; air was being forced *out* of the mine. Could the spot be a mirage, some apparition created by his panicked brain? He had to reach that spot or die, and they had only seconds.

The spot increased in size until it was at least five feet square. It was real!

The roar drowned his senses. With one hand on Angeline's arm, he lunged the last few feet to the opening. They burst out into daylight and went rolling down the steep hill, barely missing the remains of a wooden platform. Scrivener came tumbling out a second later, sliding down a pile of loose rocks.

Like a roaring cannon, a cloud of dust mushroomed from the mouth of the tunnel and they were sprayed with rock fragments. Then the rumbling slowly settled into silence, and the chirping of small sparrows in the nearby brush met his ears.

Ross lay on his back, gasping for several seconds, unable to suck enough air into his lungs. He thought for a moment he might still die if his heart burst from the exertion. He must concentrate on living, and to that end he lay still and breathed as best he could for another long minute or two. Gradually his breathing began to steady, and he could gather enough strength to say: "Angeline? Martin?"

He heard them groan and mumble. It was enough. They were alive. It was the best sound he'd heard in two days.

He rolled over onto one elbow. It was either dawn or dusk. The sky was clear, but the sun wasn't up. He crawled on hands and knees to Angeline. She lay with her eyes wide open, gasping, appearing utterly spent.

Scrivener was sitting up, wiping a hand across his grimy face, looking stunned. Small rodents darted here and there and rustled out of sight into the sagebrush, as the escaped rats sought shelter.

A layer of dust coated the membranes in Ross's nose, but the desert air was still the sweetest fragrance ever. He inhaled deeply, thinking that he'd never take his life for granted again.

"Escaped, by God," Scrivener breathed. "By the thickness of a sheet of my newspaper."

"If it hadn't been daylight, I never would've seen that opening," Ross said. "And we probably wouldn't have made it."

"Blind luck or Divine Providence?" Scrivener said.

"Depends on what you believe."

Angeline rolled over and sat up. She was scratched and bleeding from several small cuts, blue dress ripped and hanging down, revealing one breast, dirt streaking her bare shoulders and arms. She brushed her dusty brown hair from her eyes. "I've never heard a symphony at the opera house that sounded as good as those sparrows chirping," she said in an exhausted, reverent tone.

Ross looked around, and realized it was dawn, not dusk. The sky was reddening in the east, and Virginia City was less than a mile away, the glare of the all-night saloons still lighting the streets. The ugly boom town looked like a shining city in the valley. He stood there, unable to shake himself into reality. Every small, mundane thing he'd always taken for granted now seemed wondrous — the crushed rocks, the sagebrush, the partially collapsed wooden tramway for the long-gone ore cars, the steady *thumping* of the stamp mills in the distance. He felt his eyes watering, whether from sudden emotion, or the irritating dust, he didn't know — nor did he care.

The men helped Angeline to her feet — and she nearly toppled over.

"My shoe. . . ."

They caught and eased her back to the ground. The thick, elevated heel on her left shoe had been torn off.

"Here, I'll fix that. . . ." Scrivener picked up a rock and broke off the other heel. " 'Tain't much for fashion, but at least you're not lopsided now and you can walk."

She smiled her satisfaction as they helped her up.

It took several minutes for them to collect themselves. They first checked for injuries, and found all were minor ones — bumps, bruises, scratches and cuts, strained muscles, and even the marks of a rat bite on Angeline's left calf.

"I have only one thing to say about that," Ross said in his most serious tone as he examined the shapely leg in the strengthening light.

"What's that?"

"That rat had mighty good taste."

She gave him a playful shove and smiled.

It was an expression that was good to see. "Not that I mind looking," Ross continued, "but you might want to consider tying up the top of your dress before we go back to town."

She proceeded, without embarrassment, to do just that. Scrivener helped her tear another strip off the bottom of her shortened dress to fashion a makeshift suspender to loop around her neck.

"I look awful!" she said, surveying the wreckage of her outfit.

"On the contrary," Ross said, shaking his head. "That painting over the bar is only a pale imitation of the real woman."

She smiled again, this time reddening slightly under her coating of dust.

Good, Ross thought, *I'm bringing her back from the horror of this ordeal.*

Both men had earlier shed all their clothes from the waist up in the steamy heat. The early dawn breeze was beginning to chill Ross's sweat-dampened skin as he cooled down. He couldn't seem to get his thought processes working. His whole being wanted only to revel in being alive.

"Where do you reckon Fossett, Tuttle, Holladay, and that gunman have gotten to?" Scrivener asked.

Ross had nearly forgotten about them. "A long way from here, I hope." He tried to calculate the time.

The sun had just eased over the horizon, its piercing rays lighting the tops of the nearby mountains and the mine buildings.

"Feel like a walk to town?" Ross asked.

Angeline nodded. "I'd be down there buried under tons and tons of rock if it hadn't been for you two." She shivered. Then she smiled and took hold of their arms, one of the men on either side. They started down the rock-strewn slope toward Virginia City.

"Don't we look a sight, though?" Angeline said as they approached the town, drawing stares from all the pedestrians. "Two half-naked men and a woman who looks like she's been run over by a freight wagon."

"We should stick together in case those four are still around," Ross said. "We'll stop by your hotel and let you get some clothes. Then Martin and I will pick up something to wear at our boarding house. After that, we'll all go to the Chinese bathhouse."

"Good idea," Scrivener said. "But let me first borrow a gun from one of the boys at the newspaper office."

Angeline and Ross stayed outside on the boardwalk and listened to the editor fend off questions while he extracted a Colt from one of the compositors. "Don't worry, you'll get the full story later," he said over his shoulder as he came out, shoving the gun under his belt. "As much as I hate to do it, we should report this to Police Chief Amos McClanahan," Scrivener said to them. "In fact, let's do it before we clean up. Incompetent that he is, maybe he'll believe our story if he sees what shape we're in."

The trio strode into the police station, banging the door behind them.

"Where's Chief McClanahan?" Scrivener demanded of the uniformed sergeant behind the desk.

The lean, mustached sergeant continued

writing without looking up. "Down at Barnum's having breakfast. He's been up all night on a big case."

"Let's go," Ross said, reaching for the door.

"Hey!" the sergeant cried, finally looking up. "You're the three they been looking for."

"What?"

"Yeah, John Rucker and a bunch of unemployed miners from the Blue Hole are down in the Dead Broke Mine looking for you right now. Figured they wouldn't find nothing but. . . . Well, you'd best get on down and report to the chief. He'll fill you in. I'd take you myself, but I can't leave my desk right now." The sergeant stood up and came around the desk as if he wanted to be in on the action, but couldn't take a chance on vacating his assigned station.

"By the bones o' me ancestors!" Chief Amos McClanahan heaved his bulk from his chair, bloodshot eyes bulging. Coffee slopped out of his mug as he jarred the table. "Look who's draggin' in here after we spent the night lookin' for your remains!"

As they approached the chief's restaurant table, Ross couldn't tell if the lawman's reaction was anger, or just complete surprise.

"Somebody run up to the Dead Broke

Mine and call off the search!" he yelled to nobody in particular.

Two men in the room jumped up and hurried out.

Ross was beginning to feel the effects of his ordeal. He held a chair for Angeline, and then dropped into one next to her. Scrivener remained standing.

It wasn't until that moment that Ross received a sudden jolt. Frank Fossett was sitting at the chief's table. Ross was still foggy. This was some delusional reaction conjuring up a vision of his tormentor. Ross heard a sharp intake of breath beside him as Scrivener yanked his borrowed pistol and cocked it.

Belying his size, McClanahan sprang forward and hit the editor's arm just as the gun roared. A bottle of whiskey exploded on the backbar, and everyone dived for cover. "You damned fool!" the policeman howled, wrenching the gun from Scrivener's hand.

The early breakfast customers in Barnum's were buzzing, looking and pointing. Some edged closer to hear what was being said.

"OK, all of you go about your business. The excitement's over," the chief said, waving them back. "If you got eyes, you can see they're back from the dead. Go on, get back to your food. You'll have the full story in the paper later."

Fossett lifted his hands from his lap and placed them on the table. Their trembling rattled the manacles securing them. The sandy-haired editor of *The Gold Hill Clarion* wore a resigned, placid look.

"He's my prisoner," McClanahan said.

"He's one o' them, Amos!" Scrivener nearly choked getting the words out.

"Hell, don't you think I know it? He came in before daylight and told me the whole story. I arrested him on the spot. But if it hadn't been for him coming forward, nobody would've known where you were or what happened. He also turned in a Navy Colt and a little Thirty-Two cartridge pistol he claims he took off you." He motioned for all of them to pull up closer to his table. Then he sat down heavily himself and signaled the waiter for more coffee. "By God, you look like you been clawed by a mountain lion," he said, eyeing the three a little closer.

Angeline was shivering in the strapless dress, leaning forward and hugging herself. The chief stripped off his big, blue uniform coat and handed it to Scrivener. "Put this around her."

The editor complied and she gave McClanahan a grateful smile.

"OK, let's hear your side of it," the chief said, rubbing his puffy red eyes.

"I told you what happened, Chief," Fossett said in an exasperated tone.

"You keep quiet," McClanahan said, waving a beefy hand at his prisoner. "I want to see if their story fits with yours."

"Ross and I were leaving the *Enterprise* office about half past one in the morning," Scrivener began. "We ran into Angeline on the street and offered to walk her home. A Washoe zephyr was blowing like hell, but we felt, or heard, an explosion nearby as we passed the Wells, Fargo office. . . ." He went on to detail their discovery of the robbery in progress, followed by the gun battle. Ross added a detail now and then from his own perspective.

"Three men were wounded," Fossett said.

"You already told me that," the chief said. "I told you to be quiet and let them talk."

Ross took up the tale and Angeline put in a comment or two as he went along. McClanahan listened intently to the harrowing story that concluded with the race for their lives. "Hadn't been for Martin knowing how most of those mines have an inclined tunnel dug down under the body of ore, we wouldn't have made it," Ross finished.

The chief puffed his cheeks and let out a low whistle of amazement. "Yep, that squares with what Fossett said, so I reckon he told me the truth. Now it's just a matter of finding Tuttle, Slater, and Holladay."

Scrivener eyed Fossett. "As one editor to another, why'd you turn on them? Didn't they pay you enough? No honor among thieves and murderers?" The vitriol dripped from his voice.

Fossett retained his calm demeanor. "Martin, you and I have had our differences. I admit you got me so riled up, I torched your office. But I'm not a sneak thief or killer. When I hooked up with those two, I did it 'cause I needed the money, and that's all. Things began to get out of hand, what with robbery and murder and plotting to force Wells, Fargo to sell out their stage line. It was way more than I ever bargained for. I had a personal grudge against you and Clemens for that stuff you wrote about me, but I'm a decent man, and never intended to hurt anyone." He turned to Ross. "You shot me, and I reckon I had it coming. But I was only trying to put the newspaper out of business. There's a big difference between destroying a man's business and taking his life. I have a wife and child at home. They're not proud of what I did. But I reckon I'm trying to make amends. When they put you three down that mine shaft, it was the last straw for me. I slipped away and came straight to the police."

Ross said nothing, but reflected that he never ceased to be amazed by human nature.

The chief jerked his head toward Fossett. "He'll be charged and go to trial. But, considering the circumstances, I'd guess he'll be let off easier. I'll testify. Why he came in of his own accord, I don't know. Maybe revenge, jealousy, or guilty conscience. But the fact remains he did confess and pointed the finger at his former partners."

"You said someone is down in the mine, looking for us?" Ross said.

"I rousted out the president of the miners' union and he rounded up John Rucker and several men who'd quit the Blue Hole. They volunteered to try to find you. They're searching now." He scrubbed a hand across his unshaven jowls. "I been up there at the hoisting works the last few hours myself, waiting for word. The news spread around town, and everybody's been pulling for you to be rescued. First thing Rucker found was that collapsed tunnel at the bottom of the shaft where you went in. Figured you'd been buried by the blast. Some of the miners were digging for your bodies there, while others took horns and whistles and lanterns and started searching the other tunnels and other levels. But there're miles of passageways below that mountain." He shook his head. "If you'd stayed put at the bottom of the main shaft, they'd have snaked you outta there in two shakes of a lamb's tail."

"We didn't know anybody'd come looking, because nobody knew we were down there," Scrivener said. "We had to try to save ourselves."

"And, by Jesus, you did it . . . with a little help from the Almighty."

"He could've helped without scaring my hair grayer than it already is," Scrivener said.

"What about Crawford, the Wells, Fargo agent?" Ross asked.

"Wounded, tied, and gagged. He'll be all right. Fossett, here, takes credit for the man not being killed. Anyway, that's what he claims."

"I saw no reason to kill the man," Fossett said. "He didn't see our faces before we jumped him, so he couldn't identify anyone later."

"I don't blame you for trying to save your neck from the gallows," the chief said to

Fossett. "And it'll go in your favor that you told us where to find the bullion and coin that was looted."

"Where was it?" Ross asked.

"In Ben Holladay's stage stable between here and Carson City."

"Nobody was guarding it there?" Scrivener asked.

"Nope. Fossett said the plan was to leave it hid for a day or two under a haystack until things cooled down, then move it out under cover of night a little at a time."

"So Tuttle and Slater and Holladay are gone?"

The chief nodded. "We have a man at Tuttle's mansion in Carson City, but he hasn't shown up there yet. And you can bet Holladay will have an alibi that he was in Colorado or somewhere else when all this happened. Except for Fossett's testimony . . . and your eyewitness accounts, of course . . . some lawyer will have a tough time proving Ben Holladay had any connection at all with these robberies and killings. But, if he's apprehended, your sworn testimony might sway a jury."

"Why did you rob the Wells, Fargo office instead of sticking to the stagecoach hold-ups?" Ross asked Fossett.

"Holladay figured it was taking too long

and getting too many of his men shot so he decided to go for the big haul . . . try to bring Wells, Fargo to their knees in a hurry."

"I wouldn't be for doin' so much talking," Chief McClanahan advised. "Save it for your trial."

"Doesn't matter. I'll say the same thing on the stand. When I decided to come to you, I intended to make a clean breast of the whole thing. I'll tell the simple truth as I know it. Won't try to hide anything. I had a good record up to now. I'll take whatever's coming to me."

Ross wondered if this was the same defensive, arrogant man he'd confronted in front of the *Clarion* newspaper office only recently. People could, and did, change. Fossett might have been putting up a front that day. Or he could be putting up one now. No, the man's actions spoke louder than any words. And what he'd done, for whatever reason, would probably save him from the hangman.

A few minutes later, McClanahan stretched and stood up. He handed Scrivener back his gun. "Keep that thing quiet, or you'll be my next guest." He took Fossett by the arm. "I'll be returning m' prisoner to the lockup. He'll be under guard for his own protection."

"From what?"

"Oh, he's a marked man now, after turning on his partners. I figure Billy Joe Slater will come looking to shut his mouth, permanently."

Fossett looked sick.

Ross pictured the flat, black eyes of the emotionless gunman. *He won't be back unless someone pays him,* Ross thought. *Slater's not the type to do anything for revenge. On the other hand, eliminating the major inside witness would also protect him from hanging, should he ever be caught.* With a jolt, Ross realized that, to a lesser extent, he and Scrivener and Angeline were also witnesses, and their lives in jeopardy.

Just then there was a commotion at the door and several miners walked in, led by the broad-shouldered John Rucker wearing a plaid shirt. The stocky miner came straight to Ross and gave him a brief hug. "Praise be," he said quietly. "We were beginning to think you were gone, especially after we heard that cave-in." He solemnly shook hands with Scrivener and Angeline.

Ross looked at the grimy, dirt-streaked miners standing silently a few feet away. "Thank you all for coming to rescue us."

They nodded and muttered their acknowledgement.

"Whatever they want to eat or drink is on me!" Ross yelled at the waiter and bartender who were watching the scene. "Time for us to clean up and find some clothes," Ross added.

Angeline handed back the chief's coat, and took Ross's hand. The two of them and Scrivener went out into the sunshine of a new day.

CHAPTER TWENTY

Three days later Martin Scrivener stood in front of the Wells, Fargo office, saying good bye to Gil Ross and Angeline Champeaux as they prepared to board a westbound stage.

"Next to Virginia City, San Francisco is about as lively a place as you could find," Scrivener said. "But things are going to be almighty dull around here with both of you gone."

"I don't think it was our presence that created all the excitement," Ross said. "I'll have to give Clemens credit for that with those editorials he conjured up while you were out of town. They turned out to be closer to the mark than he ever imagined."

"Yeah. Events took a definite downturn from there," the editor agreed, stroking his goatee. "Too bad you can't stay a while longer . . . both of you."

"I'm leaving behind the painting of me

over the bar," Angeline said.

"Looking at your likeness will make me miss you even more. But I'll also remember you as that bedraggled woman with the torn dress down in the mine."

"I don't want to ever think about it again," she said with a shudder. "It's already started haunting my dreams."

"Ross, you've got a job as a reporter on the *Enterprise* any time you want one."

"Thanks, but I've still got a job. In fact, my report's due next week. Besides, I've enough notes and fresh memories to fill a book of my own as soon as I get to San Francisco and start writing it. It'll put my other travel books to shame for excitement and interest."

"You could mail in your report, take some vacation time, and write your book at our boarding house. The landlady would love to have you. You brought a lot of business her way, since you became a celebrated visitor."

"A notorious visitor is more like it . . . since you wrote up those news stories."

"Well, what're friends for?" Scrivener chuckled.

"Speaking of notorious, do you think Tuttle and Slater are in hiding somewhere hereabouts? Tuttle hasn't showed up at his Carson City mansion for the past few days."

"I think they've gone in different directions far from here. Ben Holladay could be hiding them, who knows?"

"I know men pretty well," Angeline said. "And Tuttle just doesn't have it in him to murder anyone. He may be a lot of other things, but he's no killer."

"That leaves Slater," Scrivener said. "Cold and deadly is my calculation. If either of them is ever arrested, you two will have to testify at the trial . . . along with Fossett."

"I'll be looking over my shoulder until that Billy Joe Slater is behind bars," Angeline said. "He gives me the chills. He'll haunt my nightmares as long as he's on the loose."

Ross nodded. "She's right. We're a danger to him at least as witnesses to attempted murder. If he got a chance, he'd think no more of killing us than he would stepping on a couple of bugs." He looked at Angeline. "That's why we're traveling together to San Francisco . . . mutual protection. We can watch out for each other."

Scrivener gave him a skeptical look.

"I have his Thirty-Two in my reticule," she said, catching hold of her broad-brimmed straw hat in a sudden breeze. "Never thought I'd have to take to carrying a gun to protect myself."

"I'm more worried about you protecting

that peaches-and-cream complexion from this summer sun." Scrivener smiled, leaning over and kissing her on the cheek.

Ross tried to erase from his mind the fact that she made a very good living as a high-priced prostitute. He was probably old-fashioned, but he somehow couldn't equate her demeanor and her classy bearing with her choice of profession.

"Let's get aboard, folks!" the stage driver called. "We got a schedule to keep." The driver swung up to the high box and settled in beside the shotgun messenger.

Ross gripped the editor's hand warmly. "I might be back sooner than you think," he said. "In the meantime, watch your back. You could be a target for Slater, too."

"Hell, who wants to live forever?" Scrivener said gruffly, clearing his throat, apparently trying to keep his emotions in check. "Besides, what's life without a little excitement? A man can't live on collecting arrowheads alone."

"If Clemens is working for one of the San Francisco papers, I'll give him these last two editions of the *Enterprise*. He can read about what he missed."

Ross took Angeline's arm and helped her up into the waiting coach. Her trunk and Ross's bag had already been stowed in the rear boot. He had his fully loaded and capped Navy Colt strapped to his hip. He was taking no chances.

They settled onto the leather seat, sharing the coach with only three other passengers. They waved at Scrivener who stepped back as the coach lurched into motion.

Ross smiled at Angeline beside him. She'd removed her wide hat and held it in her lap. They had a long ride ahead of them. He'd seen her at her worst — under duress in the mine. Now he looked forward to seeing her at her best — well, possibly her *second* best.

ABOUT THE AUTHOR

Tim Champlin, born John Michael Champlin in Fargo, North Dakota, was graduated from Middle Tennessee State University and earned a Master's degree from Peabody College in Nashville, Tennessee. Beginning his career as an author of the Western story with *Summer of the Sioux* in 1982, the American West represents for him "a huge, ever-changing block of space and time in which an individual had more freedom than the average person has today. For those brave, and sometimes desperate souls who ventured West looking for a better life, it must have been an exciting time to be alive." Champlin has achieved a notable stature in being able to capture that time in complex, often exciting, and historically accurate fictional narratives. He is the author of two series of Westerns novels, one concerned with Matt Tierney who comes of age in *Summer of the Sioux* and who begins his professional career as a reporter for the Chicago *Times-Herald* covering an expeditionary force venturing into the Big Horn country and the Yellowstone, and one with Jay McGraw, a callow youth who is plunged into outlawry at the beginning of *Colt Lightning.* There are six books in the Matt Tierney series and with *Deadly Season* a fifth featuring Jay McGraw. In *The Last Campaign,* Champlin provides a compelling narrative of Gerónimo's last days as a renegade leader. *Swift Thunder* is an exciting and compelling story of the Pony Express. *Wayfaring Strangers* is an extraordinary story of the California Gold Rush. In all of Champlin's stories there are always unconventional plot ingredients, striking historical details, vivid characterizations of the multitude of ethnic and cultural diversity found on the frontier, and narratives rich and original and surprising. His exuberant tapestries include lumber schooners sailing the West Coast, early-day wet-plate photography, daredevils who thrill crowds with gas balloons and the first parachutes, tong wars in San Francisco's Chinatown, Basque sheepherders, and the Penitents of the Southwest, and are always highly entertaining.